The Broken Seal and Other Cases

New Expanded Edition

By

Paul A. Clark

First Published 2001
New Expanded Edition 2008

ISBN 978-0-9818977-7-6
Copyright 2008 Paul A. Clark
Published by the Fraternity of the Hidden Light

The Fraternity of the Hidden Light is a world wide organization working according to the Pattern of the True and Invisible Rosicrucian Order with Lodges, Pronaoi, and Study Groups in major cities around the globe.

Please visit our web site at www.lvx.org for a location near you.

DEDICATION

To my mother, Artie Clark, and my siblings,
Harold, Jim, John, and Margie

OTHER BOOKS BY PAUL A. CLARK

The Book of the Rose
The Secret Cipher of the Golden Dawn
The Threshold: A Guide to Initiation
The Path of Return
The Great Adventure
Magic, Mysticism and Initiation
Elements of Ceremonial

<u>Coming Soon</u>

The Dark Brotherhood
Practical Mysticism
By Signs and Symbols

TABLE OF CONTENTS

Acknowledgements…………………………………...…vi

Foreward…………………………………………....…vii

The Broken Seal……………………………..…....…3

The Helm of Awe……………………………...…..45

Call Down the Moon……………………………...…65

A Sacrafice Without Blemish……………...…..…87

Drums in the Night……………………………...…123

The Jewel of Khem……………………………….....151

A Question of Honor……………………………….191

Open the Gates of Chaos…………………………213

ACKNOWLEDGEMENTS

I want to especially thank my close friends Susan Monroe and Jackie Hatch for their tireless efforts in typing this manuscript (and deciphering my hand writing) for these stories. Thanks are also due to Jim Eshelman and Kathryn Downing for proofreading and correcting my many lapses of grammar (even though I claimed artistic license, they wouldn't let me get away with it). I like to express my gratitude to the fraters and sorores of the Fraternity, and especially those who have emerged from the womb of Aima. To Tony DeLuce for his unflagging support and optimism.

Finally, thanks to my wife Linda, and my sons Richard and Michael, for their support, imagination, and love.

FOREWARD

Fiction is an ideal vehicle for the communication of occult principle. Communicated in the form of a "story", occult principle is more likely to slip past the sentinel of self-consciousness and find its way into the rich garden of sub-consciousness. Within this fertile garden, true occult principle can take root and grow into the full blossom of ripe understanding. Indeed, a properly constructed occult story may verge upon the mythical and serve to bring the reader to Mysteries unapproachable by intellect.

It is not a stretch to suggest that such a properly constructed story may lead to a type of initiation. Such a story written with carefully chosen images may allow the reader to participate in certain Mysteries just like a candidate undergoing an effective Dramatic Ritual.

The follow stories written by Dr. Paul A. Clark are most entertaining and shed light upon a number of occult principles. In the tradition of Dion Fortune's "The Secrets of Dr. Taverner", Paul embodies little-known aspects of occult psychology in the form of fiction. Dion Fortune claimed that she used fiction to publish such aspects because if they were published as non-fiction "they would have no chance of hearing."

While reading these stories you may begin to feel like you really know some of the characters. This feeling may be due, in part, to Paul's skilled use of character development; or it may be due, in part, to a realization that these characters have a life of their own; in any case, you are sure to be entertained.

Enjoy!

Tony DeLuce
Huntington Beach, CA
October 12, 2001

The Broken Seal

New Expanded Edition

THE BROKEN SEAL

From time to time, one of those extraordinary individuals, known in the Western Esoteric Tradition as a senior adept, comes to the attention of those outside the fraternities to which they belong. The Comte De Saint Germaine was one, Dion Fortune another; but these cases are indeed rare. Most of these men and women, whose attainments border on the miraculous, are unknown outside of their circle of carefully picked associates. Thus, they remain largely, if not completely, anonymous unless by virtue of providence, destiny or what some refer to as karma, one is brought into their sphere of activities. It was my good fortune to gain the confidence of the man whose activities I chronicle here.

The manner of our meeting was common enough. It was through our vocation. I wonder how many of us really know our co-workers? We may go camping, bowling, or play golf and drink beer together; but do we really know about the fire that animates them? What their special talents and skills are? What makes them unique? Modern lives are so full that many are satisfied to live on the surface of existence, sampling the current trends and fads, put in their forty-hour workweek and relax in front of the television. It seems to be enough for some to pursue the goals of financial security, sex and acceptable comfort according to Maslow's hierarchy. To some, however, the powers that direct this play of manifestation thrust upon us events and circumstances that demand that we plumb deeper into what motivates our comrades and us.

I like to think of myself as one of these 'miners' for the reasons for existence and consider myself an intellectual; that is, one who searches for the quality of being beyond good wine and a good book. Until peculiar circumstances threw me into a close relationship with a unique individual and allowed me to see beneath his veneer, I was being generally sophomoric.

My name is Michael Richardson. I am one of those fortunate people who are able to combine vocation with my avocation. I am a professor of comparative religion at a small university located on the outer fringe of Los Angeles in Southern California. My passion for my subjects, together with the comparatively small size of our faculty, conspired to bring me to the faculty center with one of my co-workers for many occasions of chess and conversation. His name was Dr. Arthur Alexander, Professor of Clinical Psychology. In him, I found someone with whom I could share my thoughts on comparative religion and obscure mystical systems. Even though his professed expertise was in another field, the breadth and depth of his knowledge in my field was astonishing. No matter which system I discussed, he would amaze me with the detailed familiarity of one who is not only well-read, but who has traveled to obscure and exotic places and possesses experiences of those things others only theorize about.

Arthur Alexander looked to be about forty years old,

about ten years my senior; but many times during our association I was presented strong circumstantial evidence that he was far older than he looked. I knew he believed in the soul sequentially experiencing many bodily lives; that is, reincarnation. I often wondered if his vast esoteric as well as secular knowledge of life might be based upon a recovery of the memories of his other existences. Perhaps this was my rationalized attempt to explain why he knew so much more that I.

Physically, he was a little over six feet tall and of medium build, in excellent condition and with cat-like reflexes. He was pleasant looking with a ready smile that could instantly melt any resistance and inspire trust in most people at first meeting. I found him to be a man of the highest ethics, yet his ethical code wasn't based upon the mores of the herd. Instead, he acted from an internal code that was based upon a perception of cosmic law at work. For example, although he always dressed in the best of taste, his clothing was also impeccably appropriate. In fact, the same rule of 'tastefully appropriate' could be used to describe all of his conduct. He stated that he always acted in line with a rule that included dressing and acting in accordance with the country he was residing in. He remarked to me about the various religious cults around Los Angeles that made a great show of outward trappings: haircuts, robes, shoes or lack of them; and how they were doing exactly that, making an outward show, "It takes more than unwashed feet and a begging bowl to make one holy."

The most singular feature of his appearance, apart from the indefinable sense of inner power and strength that would give support to all around him, was his eyes. They were light gray in color and gave the impression that they could either see into the mystical heights of the misty future, or penetrate into the arcane depths of your soul. He had the unnerving habit of appearing to look behind you, which I learned was a technique initiates used to view a person's aura.

In my office one evening, Arthur and I were discussing the differences between the trigrams of the I CHING as they are presented in classical Chinese literature and those presented in the writings of the late Aleister Crowley, when I was informed that my cousin Roderick was on the telephone. Roderick was involved in real estate and the restoration of old buildings. The call surprised me, because I knew that my cousin was working in a small village in the north of England on the remodeling and modernization of a 15th Century manor house, which had been purchased by an American science-fiction and fantasy writer in fulfillment of her dream to live in the land where many of her stories were set. I remembered that he had written to tell me that the house had once been attached to an abbey, but that the abbey had been torn down when King Henry had decided to customize the church for his own purposes. He had been extremely excited about this project, but I could sense the strain and anxiety coming across the line as he spoke.

He prefaced his request by explaining that he was

seeking my advice because he knew I was better read than anyone else in our family in what he (jokingly in the past, but not now) referred to as "matters esoteric." Also, I had known him from childhood, and I knew that he wasn't one who was given to wild flights of fancy. Besides, he didn't know where else to turn. The more he pondered his problem, the greater the inner urge became — almost like a voice —that directed him to call me. He agreed to let me put his call on my speaker phone after I explained that I had with me a colleague who was much more erudite in these areas of study and who might be willing to lend some advice. Arthur and I listened to his story with growing apprehension and astonishment.

The restoration had been proceeding much as had been predicted. The plumbing brought up to modern standards and the conversion to electricity was in progress. The problems had occurred when the sewer lines to the septic tank were being excavated in the basement. An unsuspected passageway led to the sealed doorway of a sort of a sub-basement.

"What do you mean, exactly, sealed doorway?" Arthur asked, leaning forward.

"Well, two things, actually," answered Roderick. "Firstly, the edges of the door were fitted with wax all the way around. And second, upon the door itself was a circular disk of wax—a sort of seal. I took it to be a crest of some type."

"Could you please describe it?" asked my colleague,

very intently.

"It was about four inches in diameter with a design of straight lines with symbols, surrounded by two circles. Between the circles was some kind of inscription. I believe it was in Hebrew."

"You say 'was'?" I asked.

"Well, it still is, sort of. When we forced the door open, the seal, or whatever it was, fell off and broke into two pieces."

"I see," commented Arthur, looking at the telephone speaker thoughtfully.

My cousin continued: "It's almost as if we had opened some old Egyptian tomb and incurred a curse. Behind the door we discovered a workroom or laboratory of sorts. There were oddly shaped glass containers, shelves of jars filled with herbs and other substances I have not taken the time to identify. Oh, and there was a crude furnace with bellows. On the other side of the room was a small bookshelf with five or six very old books and a few manuscripts. There was a reading stand containing a large vellum-bound book with a lock on it — just like in the movies. It was very intriguing."

"But you haven't heard the best, or the worst, depending upon your persuasion. The workshop had a doorway opposite the one we entered that we explored next. It proved to be an octagonal-shaped room about eighteen feet across and, Mike, I'll send you pictures of this, but on the floor was this brightly-colored circle with a lot of symbols and letters. There was a picture of a yellow snake running around the circle, with a lot of words in a strange alphabet! Over in one corner of this room was another brightly colored figure — at least, these were apparently bright once. With the dust and time, they've faded quite a bit; but you can still see the colors."

"Where was I?" he muttered distractedly. "Oh, yes. On the floor in one of the corners was this large triangle with more symbols and letters. At least I can recognize these letters, but the words didn't make sense." As he was relating this, he had begun to talk faster, his agitation becoming more obvious. My concern was mounting.

"There was another door, across this room, and that's where we found him!"

"Found whom?" Alexander asked with a calm, intense voice.

"Simon Cominius!" Roderick exclaimed. "Or at least, his grave. You see the room adjoining was a crypt, of sorts. His sepulcher was right in the middle with his name inscribed in the lid: Magus Simon Cominius!"

"Did you open the sepulcher?" Arthur asked
.

"No! We're not archaeologists or grave robbers. On his

sepulcher was a seal identical to the one we found on the door. I didn't want to take the chance that this one might be broken, so I carefully pried it loose for safe-keeping."

"Alexander leaned forward intently. "When did this occur?"

"About a month ago. That's when our problems began to happen, I guess."

"What kind of problems?" I asked.

Roderick cleared his throat, hesitating. "Come on, man! You've made a trans-Atlantic phone call. You're obviously agitated. What are you trying to hide?" I said
.

 "Now, Mike," he answered, "You don't realize the stress this has put us under! We all feel like we've walked into an episode of 'The Twilight Zone.' First, there were the lights, and..."

 "What kind of lights?" I asked.

 "Two or three nights after we discovered the vault and laboratory, we started getting reports from the workmen and villagers of glowing balls of light, about four to five feet in diameter, moving close to the ground. I've seen them myself, out on the moors and, occasionally, at the old cemetery; always in the early hours of the morning."

"One of these globes was reported to have entered a

small farm house on the outskirts of the village. The next morning, a little boy in that household took very sick. The doctor diagnosed a severe case of anemia. Since then, three other children have had similar attacks. It's a regular epidemic!"

"What steps have you taken, in regards to these incidents?" asked Alexander.
"At first, nothing," responded Roderick. "The lights were merely curious. They attracted a few tourists even. After the children became ill, the more superstitious or, as I now think, the more aware, called in the local priest. Beyond visiting the families and the children, he did nothing. He stated he wasn't going to get involved in any 'mumbo jumbo' and make the church and his office the object of laughter or ridicule!"

"A very enlightened attitude," commented Alexander, cynically.

"We even had a representative from the local chapter of the Society for Scientific Inquiry into Psychic Phenomenon put in an appearance. He came in with a rather pompous and self-assured attitude and set up his equipment all over the cemetery. For the first three nights, nothing happened; and then, well, he's in a coma at the local hospital."

"How long ago was this?" asked Alexander.

"About a fortnight," Roderick answered.

"Just when the moon tides changed," Arthur quietly stated.

Roderick burst forth, "I know it will be a lot of trouble, but Mike, could you please come over and see if you can help me out of this — this nightmare? I'm at my wits end. I haven't slept in three days. There seems to be an evil hovering over us. I don't have anyone else I can turn to."

I looked at Alexander, and he silently nodded acceptance. "Meet us at Heathrow on Wednesday. I will wire you the flight time," I said.

Roderick's sigh of relief was audible. "I know it will work out now. You've told me about Dr. Alexander's expertise. We certainly can use it. I'll meet you at Customs."

Without another word, he hung up.

I hung up with a long, low whistle and turned to my companion: "What in the world has he gotten himself into?"

"He's in over his head, for sure," replied Alexander. "We need to have some research done. Could you come over to my place on Saturday night — say, about 9 p.m.?"

I answered in the affirmative, and Alexander took his leave for home. Oddly enough, I slept soundly Friday night. There was a dream where Alexander and I chased glowing globes of light around deserted cemeteries. We chased them with tennis rackets! I guess my weekly doubles match with my fiancé, Linda, and our friends Cheryl and Bob contributed to that twist. During our Saturday morning game, I contemplated with anticipation what would await me at Alexander's house the coming evening. I'll admit that my game suffered somewhat, but then, our game was hardly professional. For example, I would tell Linda to keep her eye on the ball when she had missed it "I did keep my eye on it! It went right back there," she would answer me, pointing to our foul line and laughing.

But evening did finally arrive and after dining at a small beer/gourmet hamburger establishment just off campus known as 'The Library' (I often wondered how many kids told their parents they were going to 'The Library' to study), I eagerly set off for my rendezvous. The sunset found me turning into the circular cobblestone drive at Dr. Alexander's rambling, restored hacienda with its small fountain and statue of 'The Hermit.' Alexander met me as I was walking up to the front door.

"Michael," he started as we walked into his library, "I know that we share a common, abiding interest in the subjects of metaphysics, mysticism, and the occult and that from time to time I've shared with you experiences and insights about those subjects. What I am going to discuss with you now must remain between us in the utmost confidence. I know I can rely on your discretion, but even with my respect for you, I would not, under normal circumstances, be allowed to share with you the information I am about to disclose. Only because there are lives in danger and also a great risk of the spread of a spiritual contagion that is pure evil. I must confide in you in order to maximize our chances for success and also for your own safety."

"Much of the knowledge and skill that I am fortunate enough to have acquired in the areas of our common interests is the result of long years (for I am much older than you or our mutual friends have thought) of disciplined application of procedures and teachings whose existence is all but unknown to most people. Access to this carefully guarded knowledge comes only after one is admitted to one of the genuine esoteric, initiatory fraternities. And this only after one has been thoroughly tested and tried to ascertain that there is no hint of ego or power drives that would tempt one to turn this powerful knowledge to selfish or evil ends that admission is granted. I cannot tell you much at this time concerning the fraternity to which I belong; save to say we are pledged to fight spiritual evil and abuse of the secret knowledge, wherever we find it. This case involving your cousin is just such an instance.

"You are going to take up the crusade?" I asked.

"Yes, but we need more information; and I am going to need your assistance to get it."

"How may I help?" I asked, wondering if we had the time needed for library and on-line research.

"I'm going to contact one of my fellow members in Great Britain. She is currently on a retreat in Scotland and would be very hard to reach by conventional means. Her assistance is critical, so I'll have to try to contact her via the 'Inner Planes.'"

"This is beyond my experience. I've read about such things in Dion Fortune's writings, but I've never really met anyone who could do that. I'm not even sure that I believed it could be done!"

"It can be done," responded Alexander. "You see, at a certain level of the mind, we are all united. What affects one, influences all. We in the esoteric fraternities have simply extended the application of this fact in various ways."

"What ways?" I asked.

"Of that, since you are still outside, I may say very little. Let it suffice to say that we are trained in ways to focus our attention on the subjective levels of our consciousness through symbols and long practice until we contact the applicable level. Then we send a desire-energized call into the collective unconscious."

"What must I do?" I inquired.

"I need you to stay with me, here, and to act as a recorder, since sometimes 1 might not be able to remember all of the details."

We waited until the surrounding neighborhood had settled down. After he judged it to be sufficiently quiet, Arthur stretched himself out upon the oversized couch in his library. His posture was curiously contained, but completely relaxed. He lay, on his back, hands folded across his solar plexus, his legs crossed at the ankles, left over right. I watched him as he settled into a relaxed state. I knew he was systematically tensing and relaxing each voluntary muscle. His breathing became slow and regular: breathe in for four counts; hold two, out for four counts, hold two. I observed him pass from a light sleep into the first stages of trance. A slow hissing exhalation marked this transition. His mouth twitched as stray memories of this and prior lives animated his lips. Then he moved to a deeper level as another sibilant breath issued from his lips. I sensed the change just before I heard the whistling bell-like sound issue from his lips. I leaned forward, fascinated by this phenomenon I was witnessing. Still in trance, he spoke:

"Yes, yes, I am trying to reach the Preceptor of the Order for Britannia. It is on urgent Second Order business. Yes, it is the Steward who is calling — yes."

He evidently was in contact with his intended correspondent.

"Greetings from the Council of the Pentalpha! Cara Greatly Honored Soror."

Then I jumped as a feminine voice of British accent

came from my companion's throat!

"And my greetings to you, my Most Greatly Honored Frater who dwells at the Mystic Mountain!"

His tone softened to familiarity now as he spoke. "Well, Margaret, I shall be seeing you again soon. But first, I'm afraid I must ask you to research your temple archives for me. I need some historical background material."

The voice again switched to the feminine: "What information do you need, Arthur?"

"Anything we have concerning a man named Simon Cominius. He lived in the fourteen or fifteen hundreds in the north of England. He was probably an alchemist and sorcerer."

"All right. How soon do you need this information? Should I send it by mail or fax it to you?" (I was amazed at the ease with which these mystics could switch, depending on the occasion, from age-old esoteric means to modern technology.)

"Neither," Arthur's voice answered. "We are going to be in London on Wednesday. Could you arrange to meet us at the Village of Templeford on Thursday morning?"

"This sounds rather important," the female voice answered. "Yes, I can be there. Should I bring a traveling kit?"

"Yes, I think that would be a good idea. I would bring one, but customs always gets interested in ceremonial items," laughed the voice of Alexander. "Until then, may you rest beneath the shadow of His wings."

"And may you dwell in L.V.X.," she responded.

With that, Alexander's breathing altered again. He turned on to his side and passed into a light sleep. In about five minutes, he yawned, stretched his arms and sat up, shivering. As he was rubbing his arms with his hands to stimulate body heat, he looked at me with a lop-sided grin and said, "Well, I'm glad to see I didn't frighten you away. Do you have any interesting communications for me to read?"

With a nervous chuckle I passed my steno-tablet over to him, together with a cup of hot chocolate I'd just poured from a near-by thermos. I then opened myself a can of Dr. Pepper and settled back to watch him examine the transcript.

"I retained the memory thread of most of this, this time; but it is always a good idea to have a tape or written record I'm very grateful that you were here and were willing to do this for me."

"I wouldn't have missed this for anything," I answered. "Tell me what that first part was about—mystic mountain, preceptor...? It sounded very exotic, very ritualistic."

"A lot of it is based upon ancient formulas used in the Orders for centuries," he answered. "An analogy would be our call-sign in radio. Those phrases enable us to make sure we've got the right person, free from interference."

The conversation then turned to the necessities of travel arrangements and finding colleagues willing to cover our classes. Fortunately, we found after a few phone calls that the stars seemed to be with us. Wednesday found us standing in the customs line at Heathrow Airport.

I was passed through with hardly a second glance, but the x-ray had shown something that the young Customs officer had determined needed closer examination in Arthur's suitcase. My companion calmly complied as he was asked to open his luggage. There, on top of the shirts and other items of clothing, was a case of red leather. Upon it was embossed a seal featuring a five-pointed star. The officer asked what this contained.

Arthur looked him straight in the eye and replied, "It is an article of religious paraphernalia."

The young man reached out to open the clasp when suddenly another, older man's hand stopped him. "It's quite all right, Malcolm," said the person connected to the restraining hand. "We won't need to examine this man's belongings. He is a close friend of mine."

The gentleman who spoke was dressed in the uniform of a senior customs inspector and was evidently the younger officer's supervisor. He was portly and stood about 5'7" tall, sporting a white mustache and lamb chop sideburns. He reminded me of Captain Kangaroo of 1950's children's television fame. He gazed intently at my companion, and then I caught an almost imperceptible recognition sign pass between them. We were ushered through the rest of the formalities by this bewhiskered gentleman. Presently, when we were somewhat alone, he turned to Arthur, smiled and said: "Well, Frater, I see you are a traveler. From where do you hail?"

I expected my companion to answer 'Los Angeles,' or 'the States,' so imagine my surprise when he answered: "I come from within the Mystic Mountain." The Customs officer did a double take and visibly blanched as he gasped out, "Good Lord, Sir! I had no idea that you were coming to England. I don't think any one of us in the London Lodge is prepared for your visit."

"It's quite all right, Frater," answered Arthur. "We are here on special business that arose only last week. This is not an official visit. I do appreciate your intervening with your zealous subordinate back there. In another moment, I would have had to explain what an Athame is, as well as arrange to reconsecrate it and my ring."

"Oh, he's a good lad," put in our new acquaintance.

"But he only thinks knives, or daggers in this case, are for skinning." At this, both of the men laughed, and their laughter increased when they turned to me and saw the look on my face.

It looked as if luck (or the esoteric fraternity Alexander belonged to) was going to 'make straight the way,' but when we emerged from customs, we found no cousin Roderick there to meet us. It was decided that I should attempt to call and see when he had left Templeford, and at what hotel, if any, he was planning to stop. When I returned from phoning the Abbey, I had some surprising and unnerving news.

"My cousin won't be meeting us," I informed Arthur. "It seems he suffered some type of an emotional shock last night. They found him unconscious, and he's in the local hospital."

"Good Lord!" exclaimed the doctor. "We'd better catch the next train up, before things get any worse."

We reached the hospital early that afternoon and were much relieved to find Roderick sitting up, shakily feeding himself.

"Explain to us exactly what happened to land you as a convalescent," Arthur asked.

"Perhaps it'll do me some good to talk about it," started Roderick, looking at each of us in turn. "I haven't told anyone else, because they'd have packed me off to a sanitarium.

"I was going over some of the plans very late last night. You know, reviewing what materials we were going to have to call the supplier for, that sort of thing. Then I realized that I had left my briefcase at the work site by mistake."

"Where, exactly, at the site?" interrupted Alexander. "The worst possible place, as it turned out," answered my cousin, shaking his head. "I left it in the basement, not too far from the door connecting the 'tomb-room' to the 'circle-room,' as we've started to refer to them."

"So you went to retrieve your case?" asked Arthur.

"Yes. I must have driven over to the project a little after midnight. I walked down to the basement and proceeded along the corridor through the laboratory to the far side of the room with the circle. I remember stopping momentarily to again examine the Hebrew words on the yellow serpent within the circle. I bent over to throw more light with my flashlight."

"The lights were not on?" I asked.

"No. Those lights are on the generator, and I didn't want to fire that thing up," answered Roderick. "As was bent over looking at the letters, I thought I heard a noise of movement coming from the tomb-room. I tell you, it caused the hairs on the back of my neck to stand up. I directed the beam in through the doorway of that room.

I'm not sure what I expected to see, but I was hoping it was just a mouse. My flash showed nothing except the granite sarcophagus, and then I noticed a bone-chilling drop in the room's temperature. I started shivering, and I swear my breath started to fog."

"How cold is it normally in there?" I asked.

"Usually a very comfortable 70 to 74 degrees. Being a basement, it is pretty constant. It might be cooler in winter, but we're in the middle of summer, for God's sake!"

"Yes, Lamas Eve is just, let me see, two days from now," commented Arthur.

"What is Lamas Eve?" asked Roderick, temporarily distracted from his narrative.

"It is one of the four major fire festivals of the old pagan religion. These celebrations have a great deal of power accrued to them on the inner planes — that is, the areas of consciousness," answered Arthur.

Roderick nodded and said, "I see," though it was obvious that he didn't.

He then continued: "That's when it happened. I swung my flashlight back around towards the laboratory door, and just within the circle cast by my flashlight I saw the boot-shod feet of a man! I aimed higher and cast the beam full upon a tall, stoop-shouldered man dressed in a black fur-lined cape with a close-fitting black cap that covered his head and ears. I started to speak, but then I realized something, and it was this realization that, I guess, caused me to collapse into unconsciousness."

"And what exactly was this realization?" Arthur inquired.

"It was when I saw that this man did not cast any shadow!" exclaimed Roderick.

"Where did they find you, exactly?" asked Arthur, leaning forward.

"Exactly where I fainted," answered Roderick.

"Where you were examining the Hebrew lettering?" inquired my friend.

"Yes. Why?"

"Roderick, you are extremely lucky," answered Arthur. "If it had not been for the fact that, by luck or Divine Providence, you happened to be kneeling in a consecrated ceremonial magic circle of evocation when you passed out and were thus protected, you probably would not have survived. I would suggest that, until this is over, you place these rooms, the laboratory, the circle and the tomb-room, strictly off limits; especially at night."

"Did the man you saw look anything like this?" a

feminine voice with a British accent asked from the door. We turned as one to see a strikingly attractive lady in her mid-forties framed in the doorway. She was dressed in a conservative, but obviously expensive suit of tweed, its brown color selected to set off her beautiful shoulder-length blond hair. Her build and coloring proclaimed her Yorkshire ancestry. Standing beside her was the no-less remarkable figure of a tall man of similar age and presence with an erect military-type bearing. He was crowned with a shock of reddish-blond hair and he sported a bustling full red mustache. Both sets of blue eyes twinkled above wide smiles.

Arthur stepped forward and gestured towards the two as he said, "Gentlemen, may I present to you Margaret and Sandy McLain."

I knew immediately where I had heard the lady's voice before. It had been the feminine voice issuing from Alexander's throat on the night the week before, as he lay stretched upon his sofa in trace. So this was Arthur's colleague from across the pond; and undoubtedly (my guess was confirmed a few moments later), the gentleman was her husband.

After hands were shook all around with suitable introductions, Roderick brought us back to task. "You asked if the man I encountered last night looked like someone?"

"Oh, I forgot in the excitement of seeing Arthur again." Mrs. McLain held out a photocopy of a portrait of a tall, stooped man, thin to the point of emaciation, his white-bearded face framed in a close-fitting black cap.

"Yes." answered Roderick. "That's exactly the man. I'll never forget his cold-blooded, piercing stare. Who is he?"

"You say this is the man you saw in the room where you collapsed last night?" questioned Mrs. McLain.

"Yes," answered my cousin.

"Well, the likeness you're looking at belongs to Master Simon Cominius, an infamous sorcerer who was buried alive in the 16th Century."

With this last piece of information, Roderick again passed into a swoon. We called for the nurse, who examined him and assured us that he would be all right, and then promptly shooed us from the room.

"Well, Arthur," commented Mr. McLain, "what do we have here? A malicious haunting or a vampire?"

"We don't have enough information yet, Sandy, to make that determination. You and I both would be very surprised at the last suggestion."

"Yes," answered Margaret. "The common garden variety of vampires, as presented by Hollywood and Frater Stoker, would not appear to exist."

"I've read many accounts of them, as well as interviewed some witnesses. A theory so widespread, really worldwide, seems to be deserving of consideration; but as I said before, we really don't have enough information to make a determination. I was hoping, Margaret, that your research would help us figure out what we're dealing with.

"I didn't have time to examine all of the records, because of the urgency of the situation and the short notice," began Mrs. McLain. "But, I did bring what I could find. Also, I told the archivist to keep looking and if she unearths anything of value, to send it over by post."

It was determined that we would all retire to a nearby pub for an early lunch. The good company in the presence of good food naturally motivated pleasant conversation and sharing of old times and 'war stories.' It was as if by silent consent it was agreed not to discuss the case at hand until we were in more private surroundings.

After lunch we caravanned over to the project site, identified ourselves to Roderick's partner and descended the stone staircase into the basement of the large home. We examined the doorway that still bore the signs of wax around the lintel. Arthur requested Roderick's coworker to start up the generator so we could view the mysterious chamber in ample light.

As our group of four entered into the laboratory, Sandy

asked, "There are some real antiques here. What are the present owners proposing to do with all of this alchemical paraphernalia?"

"With all of the trouble that seems to be connected with these rooms," I answered, "they have told Roderick to dispose of it as he sees fit."
"He told me that he is donating the laboratory items to the British Museum," commented Arthur.

"What about all of these incredibly old books and manuscripts," asked Margaret, as she bent over the shelves, blowing dust from the books?

"Those he has given to me," answered Arthur. "He thought I would know what to do with them."

"Arthur, this is a pretty complete set of Grimoires," said Margaret, pointing to the volumes. "Look, here's The Arbartel, The Clavicle of Solomon, both the Grimoires and the Sworn Book of Honouris. Just about every important book on sorcery and evocation, with the notable exception of the Lesser Key is here. I'm surprised at its absence considering the form of the circle and triangle of art in the next room."

"I think that it is probably in Mr. Cominius' personal Grimoire," Arthur stated, pointing to the large locked book of parchment and leather on the reading stand. "Margaret, you clear all of this library out and install it in your temple archives. I will take charge of the Grimoire of Cominius. I want to look through it and see if I can determine what he was about."

We then proceeded to the room where the circle and triangle were located. Roderick's briefcase and flashlight were still in the middle of the circle, the briefcase open and its contents partially spilled upon the floor. There, among the copies of the renovation plans and building supply lists, lay a round clay disk about four inches in diameter. As I bent to retrieve this material, I called out to Arthur.

"Look, this must be the unbroken seal that Roderick pried from the lid of the sarcophagus; the duplicate of the one that was broken when they forced entrance into these rooms."

'May I see it please? Perhaps it will help us determine what has gone wrong here," requested Dr. Alexander.

I passed the seal over to him and the rest of us crowded closer as he blew the dust from its surface and held it up to the light for closer inspection. What was revealed was a strange and colorful hard clay tablet, engraved on one side with bright colors inlaid in the engraving. The design and lettering was unfamiliar to me, but is reproduced on the next page.

I don't know for sure, answered Arthur. What we do know is that this is a powerful binding symbol, and whoever put it there presumably knew that. What information do we have on Master Simon, Soror?"

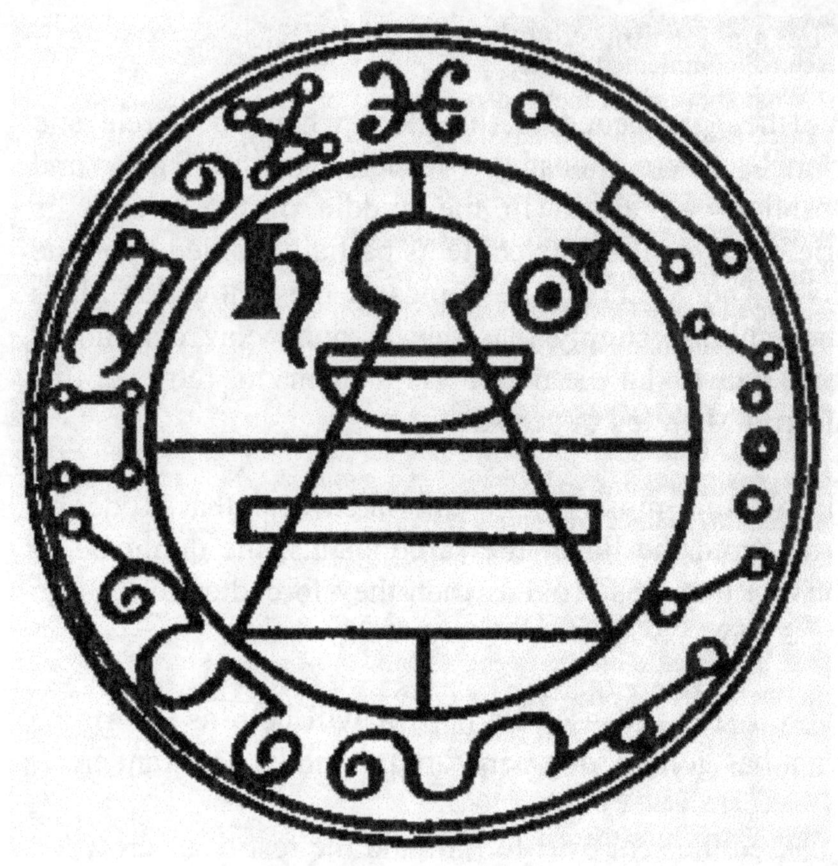

"As you suspected, he was, shall we say, an interesting individual," replied Margaret; drawing a file from the briefcase she was carrying. Examining a number of papers, she continued: "He was a zealous and ruthless seeker after occult knowledge. He traveled throughout Europe and the Mediterranean during his lifetime. He made the same mistake as the magician of Biblical fame who bore the same name. He approached the Guardians of the Fez, Morocco Temple of our Order, and tried to buy initiation. He was, of course, summarily rejected. He then turned his attention and considerable energy to the way of the left-hand path.

"After a number of years of study in this area, he returned to England. Strange and unsavory events started to occur about a year later. Suspicious foreigners began to come and go on a regular basis. Eventually, I'm afraid the superstition of the general populace started to blame nearly every bit of bad luck, from bad milk to bad crops, on Cominius. Finally, Simon was reported to have been caught, quote, 'In the act verily of raising ye Prince of Darkness, ye Devil!' by a group of local worthies supported by the moral presence of the local priest. They burst in upon him in this very room. Cominius evidently had constructed the tomb in the next room as his eventual resting place. However, it was not used exactly as he had planned."

"What do you mean?" I asked.

"The priest, seeing it, seized the opportunity of the moment and his men, likewise, seized Simon. They threw him into the sarcophagus and buried him alive!"

"Well, that took care of that," I ventured
.

"As a matter of fact, it did not," she replied, shaking her head. "Phenomena, just as we recently heard about, began to occur."

"And what was done to remedy this?" asked Arthur.

"An expert, in fact, one of the Senior Chiefs of our

London Temple, was called in by the Crown, and apparently laid things to rest. That is, until Roderick's people re-awakened and released the evil that is now abroad and gaining strength," summarized Margaret.

"And it is this evil that we are charged with defeating," stated Arthur.

"What strategy should we adopt?" I asked.

"So far, if Roderick and the fellow from the Psychic Research Society are any indication, direct confrontation has not been helpful," he answered. "Tonight, we will observe and attack indirectly."

"What do you propose as an indirect attack on our vampire?" questioned Sandy.

"We will deprive our vampire of its sanctuary," said Alexander. "As you know from the legends, he must return to the sarcophagus in the next room before the sun rises. The bright light of the sun should rapidly disperse the etheric double — the animating and true vehicle of the vampire. We will keep watch just outside the house tonight and see if our black-cloaked friend makes his nightly expedition. Under no circumstances will we confront or otherwise make known our presence. I want to choose our battleground so that we have the advantage. This can be very dangerous; let no one underestimate our adversary.

"Once we are sure of his exit, we meet in the tomb room

and cast a circle of protection about the sarcophagus, cutting off his retreat. We shall then resume our vigil outside and await his arrival. He should return just before dawn. His attention will be focused on reaching his sanctuary before sunrise, so he should not notice us unless we draw attention to ourselves. When he cannot breach the circle, he will be defeated," Arthur finished.

Thus, the evening found us spread about the house, waiting for the specter of Simon Cominius to go forth. We were paired by twos; I with Arthur, watching the front, while the McLains watched the rear of the property. We were disappointed, however. Although we maintained a vigilant survey, no vampire shade rewarded our efforts.

As we ate at the local bed and breakfast, we were treated to the unpleasant news that the Globes of Light had been active again last night, and two more children and an elderly person had been admitted to the hospital.

"How could he have gotten by us?" I asked, "Especially since we haven't betrayed our presence," Sandy put in.

"The obvious is sometimes easily overlooked," Arthur commented. "There is a distinct possibility that we have misinterpreted some of our facts. Margaret, you contact your Archivist and see if she has found anything further that might help us.

"Sandy, I trust you and Margaret remembered to bring

your traveling kit?"

Sandy nodded in the affirmative.

"Good. Go and bring it here. I'll go check with our local priest and see if I can gain access to the local records. There might be something enlightening there. Let's meet back here after dinner tonight, and be prepared for a full circle working."

After we were left alone, Alexander motioned for me to join him beside the stone sarcophagus. "I'll need your assistance with this, Michael. If my suspicions are correct, Master Simon has a gift for us with him in his coffin. A gift that we will need before the night is over."

"We're going to open his tomb?" I asked uncomfortably.

"Don't worry," Arthur said reassuringly. "I'm sure Cominius is not a vampire, whatever else may have been said about his ethics. If he were alive or could communicate with us, I'm sure at this point that he would want to fully cooperate with us."

We found the workers' tools and set to work with a chisel and hammer loosening the sealing material around the lid of the sarcophagus. A pry bar helped us slide the lid to a ninety-degree position.

The skeleton lay with hands upon breast. We recognized the black skullcap and cape from Roderick's description and the picture we had seen of Cominius.

"As I thought," said Arthur. "He doesn't have the appearance of one who was buried alive, does he?"

"But why would they say they did that terrible thing, if it was untrue?"

"Politics and ego, I suppose," commented Arthur. "They probably put that story out as a stern warning to other would-be diabolists. Also, the local priest could point with dubious pride to the extremes to which he would go to defend the faith."

"This is what I was looking for," asserted Arthur, bending over the skeleton and lifting a medallion from its neck, breaking the rotten silk ribbon as he did so. He held a metal disk about three inches in diameter. Engraved on one side was a pentagram with the words "Te Tra Gram Ma Ton" about it. "This, my friend, is the Pentagram of Solomon. Like the other seal, it is from 'The Lesser Key'. On the back, we have a sigil — a sigil that will become very important."

After replacing the lid on the tomb, Arthur suggested that I check on Roderick and then go back to the inn to rest. He reiterated his intention to visit the church and have a look at the local records.

Roderick was feeling much recovered, and I was feeling less jet-lagged after my rest when I rejoined the others at the appointed time.

Margaret was taking a silver goblet with a crystal in its stem from a suitcase. This she filled with water from a bottle, which had also been stored in the suitcase. Then she busied herself blessing this chalice and its contents.

Sandy, who quickly instructed me in the procedure of lighting and using the swinging brass incense burner, passed a censer, together with a self-lighting charcoal and incense boat to me. He then pulled a large sword with cross hilt from the valise. It was a magnificent blade with engraving in Hebrew along its surface.

As I finished firing up the briquette, I turned to observe Arthur. He was placing the medallion that we had retrieved from the tomb of Cominius in the center of the painted triangle in the corner of the room. He then bent over the red leather case that had caused such a stir at the customs inspection station. He opened it and took out a long dagger with a gold cross hilt, a pentagram in the pommel, and a red silk thread-wrapped handle. At the junction of the guard and handle gleamed a large topaz of great brilliance. The blade was noteworthy also, for it was not straight, but wavy, coming to a sharp point. Next, he retrieved from this case a golden ring of remarkable workmanship. It was very large and also bore the symbol of the five-pointed star. As Arthur slipped in upon his finger, I saw him silently mouth a few words and, I swear, he seemed to grow both in stature and authority. The quality of power seemed to visibly crackle about him. I had no time to observe my friend further. Sandy called me back to task and asked me to join him and Margaret within the circle of the yellow serpent with the Hebrew letters.

"We are going to recast this circle to increase its potency, as well as repair any breach that may have occurred that night, hundreds of years ago," Sandy explained.

"We may well have need of its protection before the night is over," added Margaret. "Remember, this is the Eve of Lamas, and the energy levels will be quite high."

Starting at the head of the serpent, which she said was at the east, Margaret began pacing clock-wise around the circle, sprinkling water from the goblet as she did so, and intoning a passage from the Chaldean Oracles of Zoroaster, her brow furrowed in intense concentration. Next it was my turn. Swinging the censer, I traveled the same path as Margaret, intoning the passage from the Oracles that Sandy had written out for me on a sheet of paper. With every circumambulation, I felt the resistance grow until it felt as if I were walking through hip-deep water. When I had finished, I could almost see, in my peripheral vision, a flickering glow where I had paced.

Then Sandy walked the circle with his large sword, pausing to salute and draw five-pointed stars at each of the cardinal points. Each time he finished a pentagram, he would 'charge it' with a strange sounding word of power. Perhaps it was suggestion, or perhaps the ceremony had sensitized my psyche, but as he did this, I felt I could see the stars hanging in the air for a second or two, sparkling and flaming in electric blue light.

Arthur, standing outside the circle, then addressed the rest of us. "You now stand outside of time, in a place between the worlds. Your combined efforts have essentially erected a psychic fortress. Do not leave it under any circumstances!"

"But what about you?" I protested.

Margaret laid a reassuring hand upon my arm. "He is to fulfill the role of the hunter, Michael," she told me. "It is an extremely dangerous strategy, and he is playing the most risky part. But do not worry. Arthur is by far the most experienced of us all, and he knows what he is about. Our job will be to act as a transmitting station. We will draw the critical energy from the inner planes and feed it through to him."

"How can I do that?" I asked.

"Just relax and think about the affection you bear your friend. Use your imagination and picture us surrounded by light, and see us shining that light in his direction. Sandy and I will supplement your imagery with the necessary symbols and shifts in consciousness."

So we three stood with hands linked, Margaret between Sandy and I, the censer, cup and sword on the floor before us. Arthur walked over to the triangle of art in the corner of the room. Reaching over with his Athame, or ritual short sword, he touched the medallion with its tip and uttered a word of summons in a vibrating voice. He then stepped back into the adjacent corner and we waited in silence.

I don't know what we became aware of first, the dimming of the electrical lights, or the bone-chilling, diabolical drop in temperature, just as had been described by Roderick. Shortly following, there appeared in the door leading to the laboratory a globe of light about five feet in diameter. As we watched, the light faded, or rather, darkened and condensed. Dimly at first, and then with more definition, we were able to see the tall, thin, stoop-shouldered figure of a gray-bearded man, dressed in black with a close-fitting skullcap upon his head. Yes, he looked just like the picture that we had examined of the long-dead sorcerer, Simon Comiius, whose remains lay in the next room. A look of pure malevolence streamed forth from his eyes towards the three of us in the circle. He apparently was not yet aware of Arthur, standing in the other corner of the room.

As I looked at the figure, I felt myself being drawn to him against my will. If Margaret and Sandy had not simultaneously tightened their grips upon my hands and anchored me, I'm sure I would have walked to my destruction. Once the creature found he could not draw us to him, his face twisted with anger and he launched himself at us. He flew through the air until he reached the boundary of the circle. Suddenly, it was as if he had run into an invisible wall. The pentagrams that Sandy had drawn in the air flared into life. The creature howled in pain and bounced back onto the floor, still smoldering where it had come into contact with the flaming star.

Arthur then took a step forward and called out, "Berith! Thou creature whose habitation is of the seven descending steps of the Qlippoth! I call and command you by your name. Berith!"

The figure turned sharply in the direction of Alexander, its face contorting with rage, eyes flashing red with predatory hate. A terrible transformation began to take place, as reptilian skin and fangs dripping smoking venom appeared. Long, razor-sharp talons manifested where there had been hands. With a howl, it started to lunge, but was brought up short when Arthur held something up before it in his left hand. It took me a while to realize that it was the Seal that had once guarded the tomb.

"Behold the Seal of Solomon," thundered Arthur. "Behold the Seal that God has ordained you shall not pass!" As he was saying this, he advanced, step by step, using the round disk to herd the monster towards the triangle of art. Finally, with one last shudder, the fanged fury stepped into the three-sided prison. Leaping forward, Arthur sketched a pentagram in the air in front of the demon with his Athame. Then, pointing directly at the cowering monstrosity, he ordered it: "Depart ye unto your habitation in the Name of ____________." Here he intoned a vibrating word of power that seemed to echo over all of the chamber and beyond. Then, with another thrust of his dagger, he thundered: "Hekas! Hekas!"

There was a flash of light and a howl that diminished as the creature disappeared. At this point, I lost consciousness.

Two days later I was sitting in the airport restaurant with Arthur, Margaret, Sandy, and our friend from the Customs Office. The last bit of tension was being eased away by our laughter as Sandy mimicked the look on my face when I had recovered my consciousness after the adventure and found my companions had covered me with a blanket to keep me warm, and had laid me down on the lid of Cominius' sarcophagus!

"When did you suspect we weren't dealing with a vampire?" I asked Arthur.

"Well, in a sense, we were. But this was not a vampire in the classical sense. Poor Simon was not leaving his grave at sundown to drink the blood of the local worthies, but the creature we finally dispatched was drawing vitality from the villagers, the young ones in particular, and was growing stronger and more dangerous as a result. I suspected the truth when Margaret shared the 'official' account of Cominius' death. These suspicions were reinforced when we found Simon's bones serenely arranged in his coffin, and the Lamen, or medallion, bearing on one side the Pentagram of Solomon, and on the other, the sigil or seal of a spirit.

When I consulted Simon's personal Grimoire, I found that the seal belonged to Berith, the 28th demon of the Goetia. This information, together with his Grimoire gave me a good working hypothesis of what Master Cominius was up to a the moment of his untimely demise.

"After exhibiting my academic credentials to the rather uncooperative local priest, I placed a call to his bishop."

"Jesse?" laughed Margaret.

"You, ah, know the bishop," I asked?

"Oh yes," answered Arthur. "He and I taught at the same university a number of years ago, when he was but a priest. At any rate, the local priest became much more cooperative after receiving a call from the bishop."

"I found that, as we suspected Michael, Simon was in the act of summoning a Goetic demon when, pardon the expression, all hell broke loose when the vigilantes crashed in on him. The force recoiled upon him and his heart failed. Being thrust upon the astral plane with that creature would be hard to imagine. It would probably have looked like a classical scene from Hades."

"You don't mean to tell me that the thing would have carried away his soul, do you," I asked?

"No. Initiates know differently. But it would have been a terrible experience. Eventually, the bright ones would have rescued him."

"Even a sorcerer," I asked?

"Michael," he answered, "the Almighty is infinitely, infinitely more compassionate, merciful and forgiving than any of his earthly representatives have even guessed."
"But, even so, it must have been terrible," Margaret, murmured.

"Yes," Arthur went on. "With the 'Charge of the Light Brigade' of the local vicar and friends, Berith was allowed to escape control. It was this entity and not Simon who was sealed in the apartments by our long-dead Frater, and released accidentally by Roderick. However, he was still tied to the sigil worn by Cominius, which is one reason he used Simon's form and didn't wander far from the rooms."

"Although it would have, eventually, as it gained strength," Sandy interjected.

"All that I did," said Arthur, "was banish this force back to its proper place in the Cosmos, using the Seal and its sigil, which, by the way, you may have," he said to me, "as a souvenir!"

He placed in my hand an almost unrecognizable charred, melted piece of metal; all that remained of the sigil and pentagram.

"At least you won't have any problem getting that through customs!" laughed our friend from the Customs Office.

THE HELM OF AWE

We were sitting in the Ahmanson Theater of the Los Angeles Music Center, waiting for the curtain to go up on the final Southern California performance of Andrew Lloyd Webber's wonderfully magical 'Phantom of the Opera.' Our tickets had been a birthday present for my fiancée, Linda, from a mutual friend. It was natural for my mind to cast back to the unusual events that started the evening we had last been in the audience of this evocative musical. On that occasion, Dr. Alexander and the McLains had attended the performance with us.

I introduced you to the McLains and the remarkable Dr. Arthur Alexander in the story, 'The Broken Seal.' With that adventure, I was given a glimpse into the fascinating world-view that sees beyond the surface play of effects into the often wonderful, sometimes dark realm of causes.

After the performance on that occasion, the five of us were having a late night snack at 'The Library,' which was actually a restaurant that we often enjoyed. Sandy McLain was relating several stories in his wonderfully entertaining style.

"Well, what do you think, Sandy?" asked Linda. "Is there anything to the legends connected with the Loch Ness Monster?"

I can't say, exactly," he answered. "Meg and I haven't

actually seen Nessie; but once, when we were in Scotland on holiday, we were visiting the loch early in the morning, and just as we topped the hill where we could see the water, we heard a large splash and saw a large 'foot-print' in the water."

"You saw what," I asked?

"A foot-print. That's what they call the effect you see on the water when a large object, like a submarine, for example, suddenly submerges."

"How big was this footprint, would you estimate," Arthur asked?

"Oh, at least 100 feet," Sandy answered.

"And there are no submarines in Loch Ness," laughed Margaret.

Our conversation was interrupted when a friend of Arthur's, whom I had previously met on several occasions, happened to spot us as he entered the establishment. When Arthur introduced him to Linda and the McLains, a recognition sign must have been given and acknowledged, for Sandy said, 'Well, I see you are a fellow traveler."

"Yes, that's true," replied the newcomer. "I have been traveling towards that mountain for a bit," he said. The McLains and Arthur shared the pleasant laughter. Linda and I looked at each other and merely shrugged our shoulders. The new acquaintance was introduced as Detective Sean O'Leary, of the Los Angeles County Sheriffs Department. He was physically about 5'7" tall and weighed about 170 pounds. A very compact Irishman, as his name would suggest. His eyes would twinkle above a perpetual half-smile, as if he were constantly enjoying a private joke.

"Arthur has often spoken of you and Sandy," he said towards Margaret. "I'm glad that fortuitous chance, or should we say, 'coincidence,' caused me to duck in here tonight."

"I take it that your words are meant beyond the merely conventional connotations?" questioned Arthur.

"Yes. I've been working on a particular case this past month or so," explained Sean. "Recently, it has taken a strange twist. Several facts have surfaced that, to my mind, may point to a definite occult or esoteric mechanism at work."

"You mean that someone is using their knowledge of occultism to commit crimes," I asked?

His answer was a cautious "perhaps."

Since the next day was Sunday and the McLains were staying at Arthur's home, it was decided that we would all meet there to hear about Sean's case in the more harmonious atmosphere of Alexander's library. Arthur believed that, while you don't flaunt your ideas and interest on esoteric and metaphysical subjects, it was important in your private rooms to create an atmosphere that focused the imagination, and which was conducive to arcane studies. This he did to perfection with old alchemical drawings on the wall, framed Egyptian papyrus, and statues of the elemental kings and angels placed tastefully amidst his extensive collection of books and manuscripts. "While spiritual studies are from the heart," he would often admonish students, "you must not forget the head."

In this charming setting, relaxed in Arthur's overstuffed library chairs, we turned our attention to Detective O'Leary's narrative.

"We initially became involved in this case through a request to the Sheriff by Mr. James Sinclair," started Sean.

"Sinclair, James Sinclair," Linda interjected. "Didn't I read that name in the Times within the last year or so?"

"Very possibly." answered Sean. "He's a very wealthy man, active in charities and politics; a bit of an international financier. But what you may not have read, is the fact that over the last two years his father, a cousin, and a close friend have all died."

"That is very rough, but I don't see that is necessarily bespeaks foul play," remarked Sandy.

"They all committed suicide," said Sean, leaning

forward with his elbows propped on his knees.

"That does stretch the arm of coincidence a very long way," commented Arthur wryly.

"Do you suspect Sinclair," Linda asked?

"Not really," answered the detective. "He has excellent alibis, no motive we can determine, and in addition, the deaths seemed conclusively to have been by the victim's own hand. Since we are talking about coincidence, here's another bit. Sinclair's wife and sister both have suffered a nervous breakdown in the last six months. His daughter is currently seeing a therapist, who is a mutual friend of ours, Arthur."

"Jennie," Arthur asked?

"The same. Jennifer normally wouldn't have violated the confidential relationship, but her unique clairvoyance told her that her oath to fight spiritual evil and abuse of the hidden powers should take precedence. She called me and filled me in on the broad outline of the case without mentioning any names. Since I was already working on it from another angle, I had no trouble guessing who her client was."

"Another coincidence," Arthur said wryly.

"What seems to be the young lady's problem," I asked?

"Demons," responded Sean.

I beg your pardon?" I said.

"Demons," he repeated. "Oh, not the opening of the ground and sulphur and flames type; but visions of classical demons and unknown, threatening presences stalking her in her dreams almost every time she falls asleep. In fact, one of her greatest problems is that, except for once or twice a week, she gets very little sleep, and usually wakes up screaming."

"No wonder she's about to crack," Arthur said.

"Sounds like a psychic attack — or rather, a series of them," continued Arthur. "But why attack everyone surrounding Sinclair and not concentrate on the man himself?"

"It would seem that, for some reason, they cannot reach the man," Margaret answered. "Perhaps he is of the psychological persuasion that is simply impervious to these 'dreams.' Perhaps they need Mr. Sinclair healthy, rather than a shattered shell."

"Whatever the reason, it certainly smells of psychic extortion, directed by a singularly ruthless individual," said Arthur. "It would take a dark soul, indeed, to think nothing of wiping out an entire family to serve a purpose."

"What would motivate such an attack?" asked Sandy. "A skeleton in the closet that would make Sinclair vulnerable to black-mail?"

"We don't really know, yet," answered Sean. "Mr. Sinclair has been very secretive in that area. We don't have a clue on the identity of our man or woman on the left-hand path."

It was agreed to break up early, for the McLains had to be at the Ontario Airport early the next morning to catch a flight to New Orleans, where they proposed to continue their holiday with a tour of the French Quarter. Sandy stated that he planned to sample the excellent cellars and 'steak Dianne' at Brennan's on their first evening on Royale Street.

Arthur promised that he would do some investigating, using his special methods, and get back to Sean if anything turned up. When I asked Arthur how he meant to proceed, he informed me that, because of the many coincidences that had occurred to bring this matter to his attention, it was evident that the Inner School wanted him to become involved in the case. With his trained imagination, he would place himself in the meeting place of all of these events, and wait for the next link in the chain of coincidences to reveal the next step.

That connection was not long in presenting itself. Within the month, Arthur had received a call from a fellow member of his lodge who was also a rabbi at one of the local synagogues. A member of his synagogue had approached Ira Bergman, whose knowledge of

Jewish Mysticism had made him a guest lecturer at many universities throughout the country, because she had received a slip of paper in the mail.

Darla worked for the local office of one of the government intelligence agencies, and had recently received a note urging her to pass information of a sensitive nature to a certain mailbox. She was assured that, if she complied, she would be amply rewarded; and threatened that, if she did not, or if she discussed this with her superiors, she would be haunted by 'visions of demons in the night.' The letter was signed, "Loki's Son".

Ignoring the threat, Darla had taken the note to her superiors. They had been unable to trace the source and were more than half inclined to dismiss it as a prank. The mailbox belonged to a vacant house whose ownership belonged to the Office of Housing and Urban Development (HUD).

When she received an envelope addressed in the distinctive handwriting of "Loki's Son," she remembered a very disturbing dream from a couple of weeks before, warning her against opening the letter. She had carefully avoided touching it and decided that her rabbi, who had taught her mysticism and was reputed an authority on these matters, was the person to call.

Thus, a bright Tuesday morning found Sean, Rabbi Bergman, Arthur and me crowded around a desk in Dr.

Alexander's campus office. As Sean donned rubber gloves and expertly slit the envelope from the bottom edge with a small razor, a single piece of parchment, approximately one and a half inches by four inches, fell out on the desktop. We all stared at it while Sean, with a pair of tweezers, gingerly turned it over. On the parchment was a design inscribed in red ink. It looked like a series of squiggles interspersed or connected by straight lines.

"What is it supposed to be?" I asked, as I reached out to touch it.

"Sean grabbed my hand with his and said, "Careful! Don't touch! You see the stains and white residue around the edge of the paper? It might be poison!"

"Excellent powers of observation, Frater!" commended Arthur. "However, odds are, if we had it analyzed we would find that this paper has been treated with a powerful hallucinogenic drug. Probably one that can be absorbed directly through the skin."

As I jerked my hand back, I turned to look at Arthur questioningly.

"Perhaps it would be remiss not to tell our friend here, even though he is not one of us, about the mechanism and especially the danger of this little piece of artwork," said Rabbi Bergman.

"You are probably right," answered Arthur.

"Forewarned is forearmed, especially when dealing with these."

 "Michael, have you ever read, or perhaps heard of Montague James' story The Casting of the Runes'?" he asked me.

"I haven't read the original story," I answered, but I have a copy of the 1950's movie, 'Night of the Demon,' in my videotape library. I believe the movie is based upon that story."

"You are correct in that assumption," he responded. "Do you remember how in the story the evil magician exacted vengeance upon his enemies by passing to them certain runes, written upon slips of paper? Then, at the one appointed time, a demon would descend upon the hapless victim and tear them to pieces?"

"Do you think that is what is occurring here," I asked?

 "Not exactly," answered Arthur. "What we do have here on this parchment is a carefully prepared 'link-rune'. It is very probably specifically constructed for the person of its intended victim -- the target."

"How would this symbol drive someone to insanity or suicide, I asked?

"Symbols, especially traditional ones that have been used as focuses of meditation and ritual for hundreds, perhaps thousands of years, are extremely potent and have a definite and sometimes profound effect upon subconsciousness. They almost seem to have a life of their own, and when planted into the garden of our subconsciousness, tend to become centers of complex energies which will work their way into an actual condition or event."

"That is why," continued Rabbi Bergman, "all genuine esoteric schools require that their neophytes spend considerable time memorizing and meditating upon traditional symbols such as, well, the Hebrew alphabet, for example."

"In a nutshell," interjected Sean, "this is also the theory behind the initiated use of the Tarot.

"Anyone who doubts the power of symbols needs only to observe the practices of Madison Avenue advertising agencies. When symbols are presented in a way that they are not recognized by the conscious mind, that is subliminally, so that they bypass the conscious mind completely, the suggestions negate or circumvent the censorship/editor functions of the waking level of awareness. This allows their 'seeds' to pass unencumbered directly into the rich soil of the garden of the subconscious levels."

"That's why subliminal advertising was outlawed by the FCC," I asked?

"Exactly," said Arthur. "These link-runes have been altered and stylized so that our conscious mind will not recognize them. But you can bet the message encoded here would reach the unconscious levels of its target and, as I said, with symbols that have been traditionally used by the esoteric orders as centers of focused activity for thousands of years, the impact can be dramatic."

"And the runes," added Rabbi Bergman, "are just that type of symbol."

"The drug on the paper," said Sean. "would simply facilitate this 'implanting' by heightening the sensitivity of the subliminal mind while disorienting the conscious level."

"It could also open the awareness to the level of the Qlippoth, or lower astral, where the images of demons abide," said Rabbi Bergman.

"At any rate," said Arthur, leaning back in his chair and placing his fingertips together in a 'steeple,' a totally characteristic gesture, "it would seem we are dealing with someone who is very knowledgeable of this mechanism and how to apply the runes as instruments in the process. Additionally, I would bet my next year's salary that this parchment has been charged ceremonially for its intended harm."

"No bet, Arthur," said Bergman with a chuckle. "We know your training well enough to guess that you have already taken a psychic look with your subtle senses to determine that."

"Yes," agreed Arthur, "and I have also recognized the signature of the ceremonial pattern of this particular charging. The runic formula is 'Elder Futhark,' and the charging pattern is Aryan — most probably Germanic."

"I don't understand," I admitted.

"What it means, Michael," Arthur explained, "is that every order and tradition has its own method or patterns of working. These energy patterns leave a kind of signature on a place or a ritualistic object that can be recognized by someone sufficiently experienced and gifted. All false modesty aside, I possess both of these requirements to the extent necessary in this case."

"You see," added Bergman, "the Roman Catholic Church, an Hasidic Rabbi, a Thelemite, or a Tibetan Lama would leave a distinct energy pattern on a 'blessed' object."

"So I can tell you," continued Arthur, "that our psychic assassin was trained in a runic order of the Teutonic tradition, and is definitely on the left-hand path -- the path of evil!"

"How do we establish the identity of Loki's Son, Arthur," Sean asked?

Smiling, Arthur replied, "I think I will ask a Frater who lives in the Valley. Harold has made a great study of the Teutonic and Runic traditions. If my hunch is correct, Loki's Son, like most of the initiates of the left-hand path, has a great ego that demands much. I assume he has a local base of operations, as the local mailbox of the vacant house would suggest. If there is anyone in the greater Los Angeles/Orange County area showing off a supposed expertise in the runes or related areas, Harold will know."

After sharing a round of brandy, we adjourned to our various homes and left Arthur to make inquiries to see if he could establish any leads. The next day, as I was sitting in my office reading term papers written by students of my colloquium class on 'Studies in Islam,' my secretary informed me that Dr. Alexander was in the outer office.

"I was right," said Arthur after we had closed the door. "Harold was able to pinpoint a most likely suspect for Loki's Son. The individual's name is Ivan Gunderson. He is originally from what used to be known as East Germany. Mr. Gunderson is teaching a small study group out in Fontana in Rune Magic and Nordic Folklore. 'The Path of the Viking,' he calls it. He is involved with a number of white supremacy groups, skinheads, and neo-nazis. Some of the groups were recently raided on weapons violations and linked to attempts to blow up various synagogues and Afro-American churches. Ira Bergman's synagogue was on the list, coincidentally. Mr. Gunderson, however, has always been too smart to become directly involved with these activities, preferring to work through others and stay hidden in the shadows.

"After getting this information from Harold and Sean, I did some checking with some of my other contacts, and guess what? Mr. Gunderson has close connections with a Runic order that was an early split-off of the Thule Brotherhood. The Thule Brotherhood was populated by a number of individuals who later became top officials of the Nazi party and the Third Reich - - including der Fuerer himself! One of Hitler's teachers, Guido Von List, did considerable work in recovering the knowledge of the runes and applying that knowledge to many areas, including gymnastics! It would seem that the schism group that split off from them, the one in which Gunderson is an initiate, has continued to develop this knowledge, especially in its more sinister aspects.

"Since Rabbi Bergman's friend was involved in the intelligence community, I did some checking in that direction. It seems that Mr. Sinclair is also involved in this time-honored enterprise, and so is Mr. Ivan Gunderson."

"You think Gunderson and Loki's Son are one and the same, and he is using his occult training to try to extort top-secret information from Sinclair," I asked?

"It seems to explain many things," answered Arthur. "But even so, we are not sure that he is the culprit; and if we were, I am prohibited by the terms of my obligation from using my training to attack him."

"Then how do you propose to proceed," I inquired?

"As I mentioned before, one who pursues the left-hand path invariably possesses an over inflated ego. We will use his pride to lure him out of his concealment. We will need to solicit Darla's assistance. She will answer Loki's Son's rune message by pleading for mercy, acknowledging his superiority and agreeing to comply with his request for information. To discuss this arrangement, she will propose a meeting at the terrace of the Griffith Park Observatory. That should seem safe enough for him, especially with her attestations to his advanced wisdom and power, and his receptive ego. I am betting that he probably feels nigh on invulnerable. When he shows up for the rendezvous, instead of the cowed young intelligence agent, it shall be a representative of the Council of the Pentalpha there to meet him. And I shall have a gift for him."

Early in the morning a week later Arthur and I were driving up the curved road towards the observatory. We parked in the near-deserted parking lot and walked towards the terrace. As we had planned, I set my tripod up and tried to play the part of amateur photographer, taking pictures of the downtown area spread before us. In this way, we hoped I could become the unobserved witness whose job it would be to report back to Sean and Ira what had transpired, in case something went wrong.

We had not long to wait, for soon a well dressed, stocky man with very long, flowing, blond hair and pale blue eyes strode onto the terrace. He looked around, obviously searching for someone.

Arthur stepped forward and called out, "I am here as her substitute, Mr. Gunderson."

Gunderson looked Arthur over cautiously, and then noticed the large pentagram ring Arthur was wearing on his right index finger. His face became the model of arrogance as he approached the doctor.

"I see our fraulein did not learn her lesson and has solicited some support," he said mockingly. His gaze turned in my direction and he said, "You can tell your conspicuous friend that he would take better pictures if he would first remove the lens cap."

I looked apologetically at Arthur, but he merely held up a hand that told me not to approach any closer. All the while he never took his eyes from Gunderson's face. I could see he was determined not to make the mistake of underestimating him, as Gunderson was so obviously doing with him.

Arthur handed Loki's Son the parchment bearing the link-rune that Gunderson had threatened Bergman's student with and said "I believe this is yours."

Gunderson recognized it immediately and said sneeringly, "How like the incompetence of a follower of the right-hand path! Have you studied our ways so little, or have you such a low opinion of my powers, that you would think that this runic message would affect me, its creator? This link-rune was specifically designed only for the Darla. It is, as we say, target-specific."

After he received no answer and continued to glare into Arthur's calm gaze a few more seconds, a flicker of doubt crossed Gunderson's face. This doubt became a look of apprehension and then fear. He quickly turned the parchment over and gasped as he saw the snowflake-like design inscribed there in red. His eyes widened in terror and I heard him utter in a strangled cry, "No! No! It is the Helm of Awe!"

Quickly looking at the trees to the left and right of us, he backed away. He stumbled and tore the knees of his suit pants, then picked himself up and, holding the parchment in one hand, ran furiously down the hill towards the parking lot. Then, as if struck by lightning (but the sky was quite clear), I saw Gunderson burst into flame. With time for only one short cry, he was fully consumed in less than one minute, a victim of that strange phenomenon known as spontaneous combustion.

By the time we had recovered and run to him, nothing was left of Loki's Son but a pile of white-gray ash, which was rapidly being dispersed by the wind that had suddenly sprung up. Fluttering in the breeze was the slip of parchment that, as we watched, also disappeared in a flash of fire. So ended this initiate of the path of darkness.

Arthur explained to others and me later that, since he was not absolutely certain that Gunderson was Loki's

Son, and thus the perpetuator of the series of psychic attacks that had driven some insane to suicide, he had decided to use a strategy of passive defense. He had settled upon the device known as "The Helm of Awe".

"It is a very ancient and traditional symbol for defense against evil forces in the Runic system," he told me. "It is reputed to turn back the attack upon the person or persons responsible for initiating it."

"So it would only affect the guilty party," I suggested.

"Exactly. Since Gunderson had dedicated his link-runes to the destruction of others, it was devastating; especially since his consciousness was so thoroughly conditioned to the potency of the runes by his years of ritual and meditation upon them."

"I guess the left-hand path will have to find another operative and method of trying to subvert governments." I asked?

"They always do, Michael. They always do."

The auctioneer's gavel-bang brought me back to 'Phantom of the Opera.' As the performance started, I remembered the look on Gunderson's face as he turned to run, and how he had burst into flame to disappear without a trace, his ashes blowing away to obscurity. I thought to myself, "Perhaps there are 'Demons in the Night' after all."

CALL DOWN THE MOON

Faculty parties have always left me strained and tired, for I have always felt on exhibition -- on duty, Linda calls it. Cocktail parties with their enforced gaiety also left me seeking fresh air. I was beginning to believe that I was becoming anti-social until Linda and I were invited to one of Dr. Arthur Alexander's New Year's Eve parties.

Arthur often expressed the opinion that the success of a party depended primarily upon inviting the right people: interesting people; people who were willing and open to both expressing themselves and experiencing others. An invitation to a party at Alexander's hacienda meant that you were in for an unusual treat. New Year's Eve found us with the rest of Arthur's guests enthusiastically painting ceramic angels and being taught how to bless and consecrate them as guardians for our homes. I guess we forget how much fun we used to have at camp and vacation Bible school, getting together with other kids and learning how to create and make something.

Linda and I were invited to stay overnight at the large hacienda. I will always remember the conversation that occurred the next morning over the Belgian waffles and raspberries that Arthur had prepared for us. Linda and I were conveying to Arthur our pleasure and delight with the previous evening's festivities. We had particularly noticed another couple. Mary and Tony McDermott, whom we at first thought must be newlyweds. As Linda and I were engaged to be married, we were impressed by this couple's outgoing spontaneity with others, as well as their attentiveness to each other. They seemed to be the ideal couple: open to each other, laughing, tender, creative, and very much in love. Linda made the comment "Theirs is obviously a match made in heaven."

"You might have had a very different opinion of them only two years ago," Arthur said. "Tony is a former student of mine, a fellow traveler, and a friend of about five years. Their history together contains a lesson that I am sure they would not mind my sharing with you, if you'd care to hear it. It is a most interesting story."

I knew by now that "fellow traveler" was a term that members of the mysterious, esoteric order that Arthur belongs to often use to refer to one another. Linda and I readily assented to the story, which I've recorded just as he told it to us.

Tony is also the pastor of one of the local 'New Thought' Christian churches. Two years ago he was experiencing one of those 'dark nights of the soul,' a crisis of faith. He was suffering from what is now termed burnout, a profound loss of confidence and a sense of creativity drying up. To make matters worse, he had accepted an advance from a publisher for a book he was working on and nothing, absolutely nothing was forthcoming from his creative pen — or computer keyboard, in his case. He seemed to have been cut off from his inspirational roots, and like a cut flower, he was simply withering. This is not an uncommon occurrence, and many different things can cause it. In Tony's case, it was life's way of getting his attention by planting this sense of profound discontent, a feeling of being entirely cut off from the flow of creation.

The Lords of Karma had been kind enough to provide him with a 'once in a lifetime' opportunity to work out a major linking. If he were successful, he would find the fulfillment of discovering his true destiny. If he passed it by, quite likely his soul and the Lords of Karma would rapidly pull him from this life until the conditions in a future life were suitable for another try. You see, we never fail tests, but sometimes we must take them over.

Tony is not average. He is an initiate. The record of his past incarnations revealed service to the mysteries and humanity — royal incarnations — time and time again. The resolution of this karmic knot was critical for him to play his part in the redemption of humanity.

Tony had come to me, as his mentor both in the Order and in his professional career. He wanted me to tell him what to do, which of course, I refused to do. I could not pass his test for him. But I did check his natal horoscope and determined that the opportunity for working this bit of karma was coming near.

He paid me a visit at my campus office on a Monday morning. On an impulse, I asked him if he would like to accompany me and observe one of the group therapy sessions that I was supervising with my friend, Jennie.

Since Tony was an ordained minister and thus bound by his professional ethical code, I felt comfortable with the question of confidentiality.

This was a group of five women and three men, all between the ages of twenty-five and forty-five years. Some were students, but most had been referred to the clinic from other therapists. One or two of our doctoral students usually facilitated the group. Jennie or I usually observed the sessions from the room next door, through a one-way mirror.

On this occasion, the three of us were in the observation room watching the group process quietly, when both Jennie and I noticed Tony leaning forward and seeming to become agitated. This had occurred as a young woman began to relate her feelings to the group. She was thirty-two years old and had been experiencing feelings of deep depression. She was an interior designer and, like Tony, had recently been experiencing a desert of creativity. I thought at first that this was the reason for Tony's focused empathy, of identification. But then I noted the beads of perspiration forming upon his brow. Jennie noticed it and started to touch Tony on the shoulder, but a strong inner prompting caused me to motion her back. There was more here than just a personality-level interaction. We were watching the forces of the soul at work.

The young woman began to recount a series of recurring dreams she had been experiencing. She told of dreams where she had been a priestess, a priestess of the

Goddess, She painted a scene of exotic and beautiful ceremonies in ancient times. As she recounted this tale, Tony had risen unconsciously and stepped right up to the mirror. She spoke of a feeling of having lost someone, of a profound grief. Then she admitted that this feeling was without basis, for her entire family was still living. Even her grandparents were still living on a farm outside of Fort Smith, Arkansas.

"But here, today," she said, standing, "I feel that I am so, so close to that presence." As she said these words, she turned slowly to gaze at herself in the mirror, facing us, her hands groping in the air.

Tony gasped, "Miriam," and collapsed in a dead faint at our feet.

The young lady, of course, was Mary. Her name had been Miriam the last time that Tony had known her, in another existence. The Lords of Karma had decreed that they should come together once again, in order to work out this bond that had once existed between them.

Tony could not be aroused, and we called the paramedics. He had slipped into a coma, retreating deep from the shock of an old wound. As the paramedics wheeled him down the hallway towards the waiting ambulance, Mary got a glimpse of his face, and she froze in mid stride and clutched Jennie's arm.

"Oh, Dr. McCade! Who is that man on the stretcher? I'm sure I know him!" She moved closer with an expression of mixed pain, adoration, and anticipation upon her concerned face. She began speaking out loud, as much to herself as to anyone else. "Looking at him, I almost seem to remember what and who I've lost! I feel that I am closer to finding him, yet I'm so afraid. I mean, if this, him, if he slips away... Her sentence trailed off as sudden recognition dawned in her eyes. She sought the memory and suddenly knew, not intellectually, but from the heart, what this unconscious man being wheeled away from her meant, and had meant for all of her life, more than anything else — love and completeness. She started to run after the ambulance, but Jennie stopped her.

"Mary, where are you going?" Jennie asked. "You couldn't possible know that man."

"Yes, of course you're right, but... but I do feel that it is him, the one I've been grieving for."

"Perhaps you do know him," I said, "Perhaps it is this man for whom you have been searching."

Jennie looked at me in surprise. Mary turned to me, imploring, "Dr. Alexander, I must go to him! Is he seriously ill?"

"He's in a coma," I replied. "The paramedics gave us their opinion that it could, indeed, be serious. I'm going to the hospital now to talk to the doctor. Do you want to come along?"

She emphatically answered yes. "Dr. Alexander. I don't pretend to know how or why, but this man is very important to me. I have to stay close to him. That feeling of grief, of loss..." Her voice trailed off as the three of us walked quickly to the car.

No conversation occurred as we drove the short trip to the hospital. Although Jennie was not exactly sure what was going on, she was enough of an initiate to recognize the hidden forces at work and had elected to sit back and watch. When we arrived at the hospital, we were informed that Tony had been admitted and a series of tests were being administered. After I conferred with the doctor, who was a friend of mine, I was able to confirm what I had suspected. Tony had slipped into a coma, and his vital signs were dangerously low but stable. The doctor said that the tests weren't completed and, at this stage, he couldn't really say that there was anything of a physical nature that would account for this condition. It was as if he had suffered a sudden, acute shock and had retreated into unconsciousness. It was his educated opinion that, unless something was done to reverse this condition, Tony's life could be in jeopardy.

As the therapist who had been present at his collapse, I explained my theory that Tony's condition had originated in a profound psychological shock, and that if I could reach his mind, I might be able to bring him back to consciousness. The doctor was skeptical about this course of treatment, but stated that as long as it did not endanger his patient, I could attempt it. I asked if I might have a few minutes alone — to pray by my friend's bedside. The doctor said yes, that he would be just outside at the nurse's station if a need arose.

Once the doctor had left the room, I instructed Jennie to stand 'lookout' while I searched the top drawer of Tony's bed stand, There I found the envelope containing Tony's watch, school ring, wallet and, what I was looking for, a small silver pentagram strung on a silver chain. He would have worn this pendant, a gift to Tony from his lodge at his initiation, constantly. Thus, it was a perfect link for what I had in mind. So, unashamedly, I stole it!

I asked Mary if she really wanted to become involved in this case involving a man she did not know. She answered with a faraway look, as if she were someone else: "I cannot do otherwise, for this yearning comes from my deep soul. Here, I know, I repeat, know, is the lock upon the door of destiny. The key is love. You say I know him not? And I answer, I know him better than my self. It seems as if I was but lately wakened from a dream and I am struggling to recover the fleeting strands of memory. But, Dr. Alexander, I love this man, I cannot do otherwise than unlock this door!"

"So mote it be," I answered.

That night Mary, Jennie and I gathered in my library. I instructed Mary to sit in my big chair and to systematically relax while Jennie set the wards of protection. I dropped Tony's pentagram necklace into her hands, adjusted the lights, and instructed her to begin a deep and rhythmic breathing pattern.

"Mary, listen to my voice and concentrate on the necklace you hold in your hands. This will guide you upon the planes of consciousness to Tony — wherever he is. This grounding point will also serve as a beacon that will allow you to orient the two of you after your mission is completed. Relax now, Mary. Relax and seek."

I leaned forward and placed my hand upon her forehead, using my energy to stimulate and 'jump-start' the subtle center located there. She relaxed into a trance and went deeper, stage-by-stage. I matched her breathing pattern and entered into a rapport with her and, thus, was able to witness the scenes upon the Astral that unfolded before her.

I watched as Mary approached a large building made of marble and walked hesitantly up the steps. Upon the top steps stood an older gentleman with gray hair that was combed to the side. He was about five and a half feet tall and looked through black-framed glasses with bright, kind eyes. His warm smile helped reassure her as she approached. I recognized my old friend, Frater S, Keeper of the Archives of the Astral Temple.

Frater S guided Mary to the Hall of the Mists, for it was necessary for her to witness what had gone before, She must see the events that, in another lifetime, had set the chains of interactions in motion to produce this conjunction of destiny. As Mary stood with Frater S in the fog, he made a motion with his hand and a breeze seemed to blow the mist-veil aside. There she saw a series of scenes that told a story of long ago.

She saw herself and Tony as young children playing in the Italian countryside. They were playing tag and throwing sticks at each other. She remembered this incarnation. Her name had been Miriam then, and his, Antonius. Their families had owned neighboring estates and they'd known each other practically from birth. Both of them had been selected at an early age for training in the mysteries, the Mysteries of Isis, the Great Mother. Their respective parents had been initiated into this tradition, and they had high hopes for both Miriam and Antonius.

The fog momentarily covered the scene and when it cleared, several years had passed. Both had been initiated into the Mysteries and had been trained as Priest and Priestess. The scene before Mary showed impressive ceremonies of the Temple. These were ceremonies where the secrets of polarity were understood and utilized by both Miriam and Antonius. This information was used ceremonially for healing and to induce heightened states of consciousness where spiritual principles could be realized directly.

Again the fog obscured the picture. The next episode revealed Miriam and Antonius in a heated argument. Antonius had recently converted to a new religion based upon the teachings of a young rabbi from Galilee, a remote Roman province. It was said that he had risen from the grave. His teachings were based upon love and grace. Antonius argued passionately, as one who is newly converted will often do. Miriam, on her side, was not open to these new ideas. She stubbornly maintained that the methods they had both trained in had worked for thousands of years, and they had no need to change. They had both forgotten that there is only one religion, and the ways to God are as many as the breaths of seekers. Both had failed to remember that there is no religion higher than Truth. Antonius pleaded with Miriam to leave the Temple and join him. She refused, and they parted angrily, each full of righteousness.

The veil of mist descended again and, when it was raised, a festive scene of the public circus in the Coliseum was revealed. Miriam, as befitted her status as an important priestess, was required to invoke the blessings of the Great Mother upon the proceedings. This she did somewhat distastefully, for she had no liking of these exhibitions. She was here to help advance the cause of her temple by being seen by the Emperor at this important function.

One of the events filled her with revulsion. Several Christians had been captured, and it was decreed that they would suffer death by the teeth and claws of the big cats. When she looked to the arena, she was filled with horror when she recognized Antonius among those meeting their terrible fate. She stood up, biting her knuckles, praying fervently to Isis to spare her lover. She fainted as Antonius attacked a lion that was about to leap upon a child. The lion turned and mauled him instead. The fog descended again.

She turned to Frater S, tears streaming down her face. "I lost him," she cried, "lsis would not hear my plea for his life because I had prostituted my office of priestess to win the favor of the secular government for my temple. In turn, I lost the only thing that had ever meant love to me. I lost it through my own stubborn close-mindedness, and stupidity."

Frater S held her sobbing form and comfortingly said, "Do not crucify yourself. You were both zealous in that incarnation. You mistook loyalty to your way, for loyalty to The Way. In order to fulfill your destinies, you must go back upon the Astral to those broken obligations and broken faiths — back to the time when you judged each other — and seek the judgment of She in whose name you incorrectly passed that judgment."

"How may I do this," Mary asked?

"Place Antonius' pentagram about your neck. Now make a fist of your left hand. When you meet Antonius upon 'The Way', you will see he also has made a fist with his left hand. He did this at the request of the Ones of the Third Order. I strictly charge both of you not to relax that hand until instructed to do so by the Great Ones." He turned and the mist parted, revealing a great pylon gate. Frater S made a sign before this gate and told Miriam to pass through. She walked boldly forward.

She first became aware of the rich, clean fragrance of

the forest. Then she realized she was walking along a well-worn forest path on a moonlit night. Miriam was traveling in a procession with the brothers and sisters of The Way. Each was wearing a long gray robe and sandals. As she looked up ahead, she could see the path widen and a wall of living cypress trees, growing closely side-by-side. As Miriam approached closer, she could see that they enclosed a natural basin of rock, perhaps thirty feet in diameter. Following the others she came to the opening between these trees stopped and slipped off her sandals, as the others had done. She moved through the cypresses and down onto a rock ledge not worked by human hands, which stretched knee high around the circle at the base of the trees. The stones had been worn smooth by the centuries of worshippers who had gathered here. She stepped down onto the moss-covered ground, softer than the finest carpet.

At the center of the circle was a solid shaft of stone an arm-spread in width. It stood waist high above the moss floor. The shaft, Mary intuitively knew, reached deep beyond measure toward the center of the Earth. In the center of the top of this altar was a pool of dark liquid, reflecting the bright moon above. A hand-span distance above the pool, a clear blue flame burned bright and unwavering. The gentle breeze that played in the trees did not seem to disturb this sacred flame. Around the pool, the stone rim of the altar was wide enough to easily hold the sacred elements of the four quarters: a crystal goblet, sheaves of wheat, a white rose, and an earthen brazier.

Miriam sat upon the stone ledge. The others entered and filled the circle, except at the cardinal points, where a higher stone outcropping rose above the seating ledge. When the moon was directly overhead, one of the sisters rose and went to the altar. She took the crystal goblet of water to the west and raised it high and said:

"Spirits of the West, we invoke ye! Thou of the waters, of the cosmic womb, thou of eternal motherhood and unselfish love, thee, thee we summon! Oh, Thou living consciousness of the great sea! Lady of understanding, be with us." She left the goblet upon the stone outcropping and returned to her seat.

Another Priestess rose and went to the altar. She took the sheaves of wheat to the north and raised them high, saying:

"Spirits of the North, we invoke ye! Oh, thou of Earth, of enduring stability and strength. Oh, garden of abundance and nurturance, we summon thee!
"Enduring Spirit of the great mountains, thou of the forest and field, be thou with us!"
She left the wheat in the north and returned to her seat.

One of the brothers now rose and went to the altar. He took the rose to the east and held it high, saying:

"Spirits of the East, we invoke ye! Oh, Thou of the dawn, the clouds, the wind, the sky, we summon thee! Lady of the gate of prayer, Guardian of the breath of life, be thou with us!" After leaving the rose upon the stone outcropping, he returned to his seat.

A second priest rose and approached the altar. He lifted the small earthen brazier from its place. Its pungent myrrh scented smoke curled above it. He took it to the south and raised it high in invocation, calling:

"Spirits of the South, we invoke ye! Oh, thou of summer, of warmth and long days, thee, thee we summon! Oh, Lady of passion and love; oh, Spirit of glowing fire and power, be thou with us!" He left the brazier in its place in the south and returned to his seat.

In the basin, all called to the Goddess. Miriam could feel the yearning of all of her fellow aspirants, and of the trees and the unseen forest folk. She stood and walked to the altar to make the invocation. Her heart nearly stopped as she looked at the priest that joined her. It was Antonius, drawn across the gulfs of consciousness to this sacred place between the worlds, outside of time, to be with his true mate, to take this test, this working out of the pattern on the tapestries of their destiny.

They joined hands and faced the altar, looking up into the stars. Miriam called forth the invocation in a strong, clear chant. She sent the vibrations forth into the night as priestesses of the Great Mother have done through the ages:

"Thou who art the mother of all things, whose son is the

Sun, come from thy far off place and walk among us who art thy children. Come from beyond time to be our teacher and our guide. Look with favor upon she who is thy priestess, and upon he who would be thy priest." Antonius lifted his right arm towards the full moon, cupping his hand about it so that he appeared to hold the silver orb:

"Behold, I call down the Moon!" With these words, he made a fist, appearing to grasp the moon, and brought his hand down to the altar.

Miriam once again spoke: "Great Isis, behold, thy handmaiden waits for thy presence. Make me thy garment for a short space of time, a hall where goddess and priest may meet mind to mind. It is our wish to know the mind of the Mother, and that can awaken in us the knowledge of thy eternal presence in each of thy children."

The first announcement of Her presence was the quickening of Miriam's pulse. She appeared, veiled in mystery. There, where the altar had been, they saw an impenetrable midnight blue silhouette of a human form, twice the height of a human. It was as if the very fabric of space had been fashioned to take on the outline of a robed and veiled woman. Within that form, they could see stars sparkling, slowly, slowly swirling in the cosmic dance. A warm, soft, secure feeling emanated from Her, filling the circle with peace. As She appeared, the stones warmed and the current of life and growth swelled up through the trees, and up through the soles of the feet of Her priests and priestesses, filling them with awe and power.

They stood before Her, completely exposed, down to their inmost thought and emotion, their feelings of unworthiness visible for Her to see. They felt Her examine every hidden motive. She knew every time that they had allowed safety and convenience to outweigh integrity and responsibility; every time they had let fear of inadequacy paralyze their ability to embody the Truth; every time they had allowed fear of rejection to prevent them from offering love and support; every time they had succumbed to selfishness, or allowed anger or jealousy to rule over their true knowledge of the kinship of all life.

They could see all the errors of the past that had caused such pain to themselves and others. They knew that all of this was exposed — exposed to Her! They trembled in fear and shame.

But from Her they felt from only acceptance and approval. Her voice was heard in the rustling of the trees:

"My dear children, I understand. I understand what you are strong enough to reveal. I understand what you seek to hide. I understand what you do not as yet even know is within you. The bud is not yet the flower, yet the bud is as much a part of my plan of growth as is the ripened fruit."

Miriam and Antonius could see and feel the warm indigo embrace of the Lady enclosing them safely and securely. In every direction they could see only the midnight sky and its stars slowly circling about them. Stripped of all vain show of ego, they silently offered their knowledge of their limitations, and honest assessment of their shortcomings. Still they felt the Lady's acceptance as she answered:

"Glory be to the Father. It is through Him that you have learned to examine and discriminate and analyze those patterns which cause you pain. But Father's gifts are not mine. I give you my love, without reservation, without condition. I loved you when you were a helpless babe. I loved you when you took your first steps away from me into Assiah, the material world. And I loved you when later you were ready to take up the inner paths in your return to the Source. As a baby grows strong and bold, it will try to walk and it will fall many times. Do you loathe it when it falls? With each attempt, it grows stronger, better balanced. So it is with you. Do not expect to learn new steps without stumbling. The only way not to stumble is not to try. No, rather praise the steps, honor the striving, see the perfect beauty of the pattern of growth within you which unerringly leads to mastery."

"Your Father gives you challenge and the tools to meet it. Your awareness has grown to the point where you are now able to see the outer and you condemn what you perceive there as immature and inadequate in yourself. But I can see that even those patterns and that pain have served the ultimate goal. You will come some day to bless all experience, both the joy and the pain. For while the true goal was still too far for you to see, and you were still blind to the law of Karma, it was your pain which spurred you to free yourself of the chains that hindered your climb on the path of return. Many chains you have now released. Some you can see but choose to carry for yet a while, though they wound you. There are even others that you do not yet see. But no chains can bind you unless you cling to them, for you are children of the heavens, and heirs to the gods.

To understand my creation, you must move in the rhythm of its cycles. Turn to the Father by Light of Sun. Strive for Truth and study and achieve. Then, by Light of Moon and Stars, come unto me. Learn to accept and to reflect, to heal and to nurture; learn to manifest peace.

" Sacrifice to me your feelings of unworthiness and inadequacy, whether they take the form of old pain recalled and re-experience, or despair, or anger masking secret fears. But first, consider well. Would you give away your last excuse for not taking full responsibility for your life? Would you give me what you hide in your hand? Your failures, your inadequacy, your unworthiness?"

Miriam and Antonius felt their left hands twitch. They had all but forgotten the instructions when they were told to make the fist. At first, their fingers would not respond to their commands. Slowly, they uncurled their hands, like petals of a flower. As looked down at their empty hands, The Lady again spoke:

"Of course, there never were any failures! The Divine Plan is without error. Sacrifice to me then, the fear of what you imagined to be your hidden flaw, and then do not blaspheme before me. Despise not what I name beautiful. Every circumstance in your life has eventually deepened your ability to love. See yourself as I see you: growing, maturing, perfecting."

Then Miriam and Antonius felt the kiss of the Great Mother upon their brow and were transformed. The wounds of their very soul were healed. With that kiss, they felt as strong as an old oak, as bright as the full moon, and as full of peaceful joy as a cascading forest stream. They were whole. They looked up and saw the altar. No dark and starry form appeared there now. Miriam and Antonius grasped hands across the altar and recited the 'Litany of Consciousness,' each seeing in the other the perfected image of god and goddess.

"You are the Christos, the anointed One, the Consecrating Flame, vitalizing my mind," spoke Miriam.

"You are the Holy Spirit of God, the Shekinah, the Presence of Good within, the Purifying Altar, cleansing my heart," answered Antonius.

On they went, declaring to each other the divinity they saw in their beloved. They linked, level by level, from the very core of their being. When they concluded, they found themselves back in their physical bodies, searching for the other. Temporarily, they were separated and disoriented. But that was only temporary, as a hospital room reunion later that day would testify.

"So they discovered their destiny?" Linda asked. "They found each other, across the abyss of time."

"Yes, they found each other and found their destiny as co-creators," answered Arthur.

"But you haven't told us what that was." I protested.

"You mean, what their destiny was," responded Arthur?

"They served as vehicles for the birth of a very advanced, old soul. His role is to become a prominently important world teacher, one who will help unite modern Christianity with the Ancient Wisdom Teachings that lay at its root. Yes, young Christopher will certainly make his parents and me proud."

"You proud?" I quipped.

"Of course," Arthur replied, pouring more hot chocolate. "After all, I am his godfather!"

A SACRIFICE WITHOUT BLEMISH

It was a bright sunny spring day in Southern California. Overhead I could see the Goodyear Blimp gliding in the general direction of the Rose Bowl. The San Gabriel Mountains stood out in clear relief with a few white puffy clouds just visible over their summits. I had just deposited my car in the circular cobblestone driveway in front of Dr. Arthur Alexander's restored hacienda and was heading for the door when I heard the laughter of men coming from the yard area in back, and decided to alter my course in that direction. As I rounded the corner, I was suddenly confronted by the scene of two men, each over six feet tall, one white and one black, attacking a diminutive Korean gentleman -- and the Korean was winning! I would have perhaps been more alarmed if all three had not been wearing black karate gis (uniforms), or if I had not recognized the white male as my friend, Arthur.

As I watched, Arthur launched a long attack, known as a step-back sidekick, with great ferocity. In the split second of a heartbeat, the little Korean dropped under the kick, his chest touching his fully crouched knee. Simultaneously, he twisted his body, executing the sweep called a low-spin kick. This kick tripped my friend's supporting leg from under him, causing him to fall backwards, his feet now higher than his head. He slapped the mat hard with both hands to break his fall. As he lay on his back laughing, the black gentleman walked up with his hands on his hips, also laughing, and asked: "Well, Master Kim, have Arthur and I worn you out yet?"

"You need more practice," Master Kim answered, helping Arthur to his feet.

Seeing me as he brushed himself off, Arthur smiled and waved me over. "Mike! I don't think you've formally met Master Kim, my Hapkido instructor, or my fellow student, Kevin," he said, pointing to the young black man.

Hands were shook all around as I said to Master Kim, "That was very impressive! In most styles of Karate that I've had the opportunity to see, the defender would have simply blocked that kick down and then countered. You avoided the kick and countered all at once."

"That is true. The difference is fundamental to the art. This is Hapkido, not Karate. It is a union of hard and soft styles. The block you spoke of would have been an example of a hard move, where we meet force with force. This works well enough if," Master Kim held up his index finger for emphasis, "if you are stronger or bigger than your opponent. The leg, however, is much more powerful than the hand; thus, I used a soft move."

"What makes Hapkido, or the 'Way of the One Force,' unique among martial arts, is its foundation upon Zen philosophy and three basic principles," Arthur interjected.

Kevin continued: "The 'power principle' states that we should not combat our opponent's power with our own. Instead, we redirect our opponent's attack, adding just a little bit of our own momentum to 'help' him rush to his own defeat."

"There is basically just one force or power in the Universe, to begin with," said Kim. "We just move in harmony with this principle, while our opponent is out of harmony and, thus, defeats himself."

"But what if your opponent is also in harmony with you and the principle?" I asked.

"Then." retorted Kevin, "we embrace and go out for a beer!"

The look on my face must have been worth the price of admission, for all three of them, Master Kim included, dissolved into laughter. Then I began to laugh with them. After the laughter subsided, we walked over by the pool and settled into conversation over ice-cold lemonade.

"Seriously, Michael," Master Kim continued, "There are three basic principles that our art rests upon. Beside the power principle was that just explained to you, there are the principles of the circle and of the water, If you observe, you will find that almost all natural movements are circular in motion. The circle movement generates power in and of itself. As in my low-spin kick, the centrifugal force of my leg, sweeping around in a circle, creates much more momentum than would be possible with a straight-line motion of a simple trip.

"The water principle states that our attack, defenses and counters should flow, like water, into the exposed weakness of our opponent, rather than confronting his strength."

"It takes years of practice," commented Arthur, "to integrate the implications of these three basic principles into even the physical aspects of this martial art. In addition, I can assure you that the psychological, social, and health aspects produce a person in harmony with him or herself and, thus, with the Universe. Master Kim is a good example." As he said this, Arthur stood and bowed to the smiling Korean.

I reflected on what a singular recognition of attainment this compliment was, coming as it did from Arthur, a man whose past experience had repeatedly proven that he was a man of uncommon attainment.

Before long, both Master Kim and Kevin had to be on their way, and as Arthur and I walked into the house, I questioned him about the apparent conflict between being a spiritual seeker on one hand, and on the other, a practitioner of what for all practical purposes was a deadly killing art.

"It is a matter of focus," explained Arthur. "Although it is a most deadly art, my focus and, indeed, the focus for most practitioners of any depth, is in using this discipline as another tool for spiritual unfoldment. It provides a way to integrate the body into our mystical pursuits. A physical outlet is necessary to maintain balance. We otherwise run the risk of becoming a scholarly recluse or an absent-minded processor, neither of who are equipped to deal with the work-a-day world. Blavatsky went in for horseback riding, Mathers practiced boxing and fencing, even Crowley pursued mountain climbing."

After leaving me to browse in his always fascinating and excellent library, Dr. Alexander went to change and shower. I occupied myself with a copy of The Golden Chain of Homer, which I found open upon my host's desk. I had just settled back in one of the big, over-stuffed leather reading chairs when the telephone rang. Hearing the water running upstairs, I picked up the phone. "Dr. Alexander's residence, may I help you?" I asked.

A male voice answered, "Is Arthur at home?"

I explained that Dr. Alexander could not come to the phone and asked if I could take a message. After a moment of obviously anguished hesitation, the man blurted out: "Tell Alexander that Keith Harrison called. I need to talk to him. It's urgent, very urgent. Tell him it's about Alex, He must call me." After giving me a telephone with a 918 area code, he hung up.

Long distance, I pondered. I felt a touch on my shoulder

and visibly started. "How do you move so quietly?" I exclaimed.

"I think it was less my stalking skills and more that you were occupied taking the telephone message," laughed Arthur. "Who was it?"

I relayed the message as I had received it. Arthur's brow creased into a frown as he sat back in his chair. He placed his fingertips together, making a steeple, and let go a deep sigh.

"Trouble?" I asked.

"Entirely probable. Keith Harrison was a very close friend of mine. In fact, I was the best man at his wedding. I still consider him a friend, but he has made it very clear that he considers me responsible, however indirectly, for a great tragedy in his life."
"Was it involving this Alex?" I inquired.

"Alexandra? No, not at all, Alex is his daughter, and my Goddaughter. The fact is, I haven't seen her since she was a year old — at Keith's expressed request. The original problem surrounded Keith's wife, Sylvia."

"I didn't mean to pry," I apologized.

"Actually, talking about it may help me get ready for the stress I will have to deal with when I call Keith back, Sylvia was an Initiate; Keith is not. I introduced them at a party, and it was love at first sight —

definitely karmic. Keith wanted to share in his new love's interests, but could not."

"He wasn't accepted for Initiation?" I asked.

"No. Keith is an atheist, and quite proud of it. One of the traditional requirements for admission into the Mysteries is a belief in a Supreme Deity, by whatever name you may call Him, Her, or It."

"And he married this 'Soror' of yours?" I asked.

"Yes, and about a year later, Sylvia gave birth to a very special little girl. They named her Alexandra. I was the one who held her at her Christening. It was against Keith's beliefs, but he made a concession to Sylvia. I could tell on that occasion that things were not going smoothly between them. This rift between their beliefs was a chasm he could not leap. He seemed to be threatened by her esoteric activities.

"Sylvia became pregnant again the next year. Keith became more possessive, more jealous and, finally, Sylvia left the Fraternity as a concession to him. She confided to me that this, while it broke her heart, did not seem to improve their relationship.

"Sylvia became devoted to Alex. We both knew, from past life readings and study of her natal chart, that she was destined for a special incarnation. Alex's record of incarnations revealed life after life spent in service to humanity. Time and again her soul had received initiation into the Mysteries. This, of course, was another source of distancing from Keith."

"Finally, about halfway through her second pregnancy, Keith insisted that she abandon all of this 'nonsense.' Pride got the better of both of them. Sylvia moved out. She went into labor prematurely, complications developed, and both Sylvia and the baby boy died.

"Keith was convinced that, if he had been there, Sylvia and their son would have survived. I became the focus of his projections of guilt and was banished from any further associations with either him or Alex. That was sixteen years ago. I had lost track of them. There was never any communication — until this last month."

"Keith contacted you?" I asked.

"No, Alex did — in a way," he replied cryptically. "I felt her calling to me for help, in a dream. I cannot remember all of the details, but I do remember guiding her and telling her to return home. You can see, can't you, why I am almost sure that for Keith to call me, he must feel he has no other choice."

As I left Arthur to his phone call shortly after this, I had a premonition that I would soon have an opportunity to see if the three principles of Hapkido and the esoteric weapons of the Initiate would prevail against the power and ego of the dark side of existence.

When I stopped into my friend's campus office on

Monday morning between classes to see how the phone call had gone, I was surprised and concerned to find that he wasn't there. His secretary told me that Dr. Jennie McCade, a mutual friend of ours, had been scheduled to cover Arthur's classes for the next week. The week after that was spring break. I called Arthur at his home and, with only a slight apology for intruding, proceeded to nose into what had happened.

"It's all right, Mike," Arthur assured me. "The fact that you were the one to take the phone call is a message from the Third Order that it is proper for me to share with you some of the details that have developed. I was only waiting to see if you would follow up."

He then told me that when he returned the call shortly after I had left his home on Saturday, Keith had taken the time to summarize the years Arthur had missed of Alexandra's life. She had grown up to be a most uncommonly beautiful reproduction of her mother, and just as stubborn! Although he had done everything he could think of to discourage it, she had a strong mystical streak in her character. In Keith's words, "She espouses every stray cat, and underdog, down and out causes from free dinners for the homeless at Thanksgiving, to shelters for battered and abused wives."

"She told her father that she had been singled out by the leader of this 'spiritual community' by the name of Roman North. She described him as having red hair and bristling red beard, very hypnotic eyes, and as being the most fascinating man she had ever met -- at least at first. She had been drawn to this older man.

"How old did you say he was?" I asked.

"Very old, by her standards. About your age, Michael."

"Thanks loads," I grinned.

"She told her father that his teachings were very liberating, at first: Freedom to pursue your own destiny; Freedom to crush all who would thwart your designs; the power to bless or to curse. It sounded rather like Aleister Crowley, but Crowley without his spiritual side, his genius, or his sublimity. Crowley taught that the purpose of all experience was to find your True Will, but he would point out that this Will was essentially the Divine Will. This teacher of Alexandra's seems to have taken Crowley's command of 'Do what Thou Wilt shall be the whole of the Law,' and substituted 'Do what you want.' A very different thing altogether. What he didn't seem to allow for or acknowledge was the fact that whenever occult power is used to attack or influence someone, even with the excuse that it is 'for their own good,' it is a trip on the left-hand path and like walking into quicksand.

"Little by little, Alex began to see this group and its guru for what they were. The enforcement of absolute obedience to the senior members of the cult, especially the 'holy one,' that is, North; the free use of drugs 'to remove the inhibitions of the repressive society'; the frequent use of multiple sex partners to 'build the cones of power' during ceremonies; the torturing of small animals for the same purpose; all contributed to disillusioning her. The cult would require certain of the girls to solicit sex for money from individuals North wanted to influence. He would then blackmail these victims into getting what he wanted. Girls or boys who refused were accused of the crime of disobedience and were locked in a small metal building for up to twenty-four hours. Some just — disappeared!"

"Perhaps they escaped," I suggested.

"Perhaps, but the security of this place is pretty tight. Evidently, North has a connection with a pretty bad bunch: a motorcycle club with definite, strong, Neo-Nazi leanings. Alex witnessed them brutally disciplining members for various infractions of the regulations of the cult."

"Alex wasn't sure of what transpired in the ritualistic meetings of the group. They were held at the main temple located closer to town. She had not finished serving her probationary. She was informed that she was to be initiated at the next dark of the moon. She had been given a drug and instructed to take it in preparation for the event."

"Did she?"

"No. An inner voice told her to conceal the fact that she had not taken it and to pretend that she had passed into a deep trance. She did fall asleep, however, and thought that another sedative had been concealed in her food. While she was asleep, she had a dream. She found herself in a small cobblestone plaza. At the center of this plaza was a fountain where people were filling water jars. A lady, who looked very familiar, was watching her. As she struggled to remember this person's identity, she suddenly knew with certainty that it was her mother. She was dressed in a black robe, and there were tears in her eyes. She held out her arms, and Alex rushed forward to embrace the mother she had never known.

"Her mother spoke to her in urgent tones, telling her that she must escape, that she was in great danger. When Alex asked her how, her mother told her to invoke the protection of The Council of the Pentalpha. This Alex did fervently. Her mother turned and faced a gate in a wall on the other side of the plaza. Alex's eyes followed her mother's gaze and she watched as a tall figure in a black hooded robe passed through the gate and across the cobblestone plaza towards her. This man informed her that, as she had 'invoked the protection of the Pentalphian Council, they had sent him, their Steward, to aid her.' She was then given detailed instructions on how to escape. When she awoke during the course of following these instructions, she was almost caught several times by the skinhead guards, but on each occasion, it seemed as if they just didn't notice her. When she returned to her father's house, she described in detail the hooded man's appearance and to Keith's astonishment and consternation, Alex described me.

"Keith told me they had purchased plane tickets and were planning to visit me next week, when a turn of events occurred that finally forced him to call for my help."

"What happened?"

"Alexandra has been kidnapped, presumably by the cultists. There was a note left that warned Keith to make no attempt to find her, that she was going to fulfill a 'glorious and exalted destiny.'"

"What are you going to do," I asked?

"I've just hung up from talking to my travel agent. I'm going to Tulsa, Oklahoma, where Keith now lives. I must fulfill the pledge of The Council, as well as my own as Alex's godfather."

"You have to do one other thing," I told him.

"'What's that?"

"You have to call your travel agent back and book one more passage. I'm going with you."

"I had hoped you would say that."

The next day at 10 a.m. central standard time, we were looking out of our airplane window as we passed over

Mohawk Lake, the entry point on final approach to Tulsa International Airport. Keith met us at the gate. The hours of sleepless desperation were clearly visible on his face.

"God, I'm glad you're here," he told us. "I don't know where else to go. I'm afraid to bring the police in on this. I mean these people are Satanists. Who knows what they'll do. What powers they have at their disposal. I mean, you know Arthur; I've no experience with what motivates these types of people. I've always discounted them simply as kooks and morons, but now..." his voice trailed off as he began to shake.

I thought to myself, no such thing as an atheist in a foxhole.

"Don't worry, Keith," Arthur reassured him, "they're not supermen, despite what they may think. Only one of them, I would wager, has any knowledge worth noting, and that would be Roman North himself. The rest are just there to do his bidding and to provide him with a power source."

"But Arthur, Alex said that several of the girls just disappeared..."

Arthur cut him off and responded, "Yes, Mr. North has been responsible for a lot of grief by misusing his knowledge of the hidden side of life. But his day of reckoning is near. We have to move fast, though. Today is April 30, the date of one of the major fire festivals.

My guess is that Alex will figure a major role in the coming ceremonies. But we will have a surprise for them."

"Keith, you can help us most, as hard as this might be for your pride, by praying for Alex. If you don't feel like visiting a church or synagogue, I seem to remember your local art museum, Philbrook, has an inspiring garden. Go there. Become in tune with the focus of creation and image our success."

After renting a GMC Minivan, we headed out of town towards the little town of Stillwater. Arthur said that he had some contacts in the local community. I didn't know what exactly I had visualized, but I was pleasantly surprised. We pulled up in front of a small bookstore named 'The Lady.' In the window was an announcement advertising a local psychic fair, and another publicizing an on-going Wednesday night class on Tarot symbolism. Various bumper stickers, such as: 'My karma just ran over your dogma,' 'Goddess will provide,' 'Magick is afoot,' and 'My other car is a broom'; along with a wide selection of books on Earth Religion, Neo-Paganism, and American Indian Spirituality were also prominently displayed.

When we walked into the store, I noticed an impressive selection of herbs, candles and posters to go along with the books, wands, crystals and Tarot decks. A woman in her mid-forties glanced up over her half-rimmed reading glasses as the bell over the door announced our arrival. Suddenly, she let out a whoop and threw her arms wide as she bounded from behind the counter exclaiming, "By the Lord and the Lady -- Arthur Alexander."

"Blessed be," returned Arthur, as the two laughed and exchanged big hugs. "Careful, Dez, careful. People will start to talk," Arthur teasingly cautioned. "Where's your other half?"

"Dusty? Oh, wait till I tell 'im. He'll bust. He'll just rear up and bust!"

With these words, she twirled and made towards the back rooms through a curtained doorway. A few seconds later, a man in a black Harley Davidson tee shirt and blue jeans filled the doorway. He must have topped 6'4" and weighed at least 250 pounds. Dark eyes looked menacingly at Arthur as he strode into the store, followed by Dez. Then, in a split second, a wide grin appeared in his full bush black beard as he said, rushing forward to hug Arthur and literally lifting him off the ground, "Blessed be, traveler! Long time, no see!"

Arthur introduced me to Dez and Dusty Blanchard, High Priestess and High Priest of Full Moon coven. Arthur explained that these were not only his close friends, but also leading members of the Pagan Community in Northeast Oklahoma. Dez closed the store early, and we adjourned to the living quarters, located right behind the store. To reach the living quarters, however, we had to pass through Dusty's garage and workshop. There, leaning on a kickstand, was one of the largest Harleys I had ever seen. It was in perfect,   high-glass-waxed-to-a-perfection-chrome-all-shining-condition.

"What a beautiful Hog," I said admiringly.

"Now you've made a friend for life," chuckled Arthur, smiling towards Dusty.

"Talk about heavy metal thunder," I said to Dusty. "How big is that? 1200 ccs?"

"No, this is a little bigger; 1300 cc's, two cylinders."

"You into motorcycles, Mike," asked Dusty?

"No, I'm just an admirer of the exceptional in almost any area," I answered.

Dusty once again flashed his big grin and asked, "Could I get you a beer? Bud or Coors?" He held open the refrigerator door for me to take a pick.

"No thanks. But, if it would be okay, I would just as soon have one of those soft drinks."

"Coke, Pepsi, 7-Up?"

"Do you perhaps have any Dr. Pepper?"

"Does a monkey have a climbing gear? A pleasure to meet a fellow gourmet," he answered, passing me a red can and opening one for himself.

Sitting around the kitchen table in Dez and Dusty's small apartment, Arthur briefed them about all we knew about Alex and the mysterious cult. Now I could see why Arthur came here. With the Blanchards he not only had friends he could trust, but also allies with intelligence in both the occult community and the motorcycle crowd. Dusty and Dez's contacts could open doors that would be closed to Arthur's urbane PhD persona.

Dusty made a few phone calls and came up with a lead. There was a house just off of highway 244 in West Tulsa that was a meeting place for some bikers who were well known for their skinhead activities. It was rumored that this group was practicing exotic ritualistic ceremonies.

"It could be a lead," Dusty suggested to Arthur. "Most of the bikers in the area are out by the town of Catoosa, northeast of Tulsa, at the motorcycle races. This might be the best chance we have to check this place out." So Dusty, Arthur and I hopped into the Safari and drove to the address in West Tulsa.

When we arrived at the semi-rural address, we drove by and parked up an access road by some oil-well pumps bobbing up and down in the humid afternoon. The object of our scrutiny was a white clapboard frame house, set back from the road, with a large weathered barn a short distance behind it and an idle oil well, looking like a giant grasshopper in the flat field beside it. Two motorcycles were parked in front of the house.

"Doesn't look like everyone has gone to the races," Arthur observed. "Let's be careful. We'll circle around and come up from the back."

Fortunately, the grass and bush had not been cleared from the previous year, so some cover was available. We were kneeling and crouching in the grass as I started forward. Dusty reached out and restrained me. "What's the matter?" I asked. "Did you see some movement in the house?"

"Naw, I just wanted to give her a chance to get out of our way," he said, pointing to a three-foot long dark gray snake crawling across my path.

"Well, at least it wasn't a rattlesnake," I said.

"Nope," quipped Dusty. "Cottonmouth."

As I made an effort to close my open mouth, we moved forward. Soon, we could hear the television. Someone was watching "Gilligan's Island' reruns. Arthur peeked through the window and whispered, "It looks like two skinheads. Pretty good size boys, but neither as big as Dusty. I don't see any weapons, but that doesn't rule them out. Mike, you go around to the front and knock on the door. Just as they go to the front, we'll sneak in the back door and check to see if Alex is being held in the back rooms. Play the part of the lost visitor and ask them how to get to … say, O.R.U. That should give us at least five minutes."

"Arthur, you realize this is unlawful entry?" I cautioned.

"Don't worry. With you keeping those two occupied, we shouldn't get caught. Besides, they're not the type to press charges," Dusty chuckled. "They probably would be scared that we'd bring the cops."

But that was not the way fate had decreed it was to play out, for just as I reached the road and started to walk up the driveway, Arthur and Dusty were surprised by an unobserved third biker, as big as Dusty, if not bigger, coming back to the house from the barn. He had a scar that ran from his right eyebrow across his nose, down to the left corner of his mouth, giving him a perpetual sneer.

"Hey you two assholes, you want a good look?" That was about as far as he got as Dusty's foot shot out, connecting with Smiley's groin. As the big man doubled over, Dusty put him out for the count with an old fashioned rabbit punch.

The commotion, however, summoned the other two skinheads from the house. In rapid fire, they lunged at Arthur. The first one grabbed an axe handle and swung it diagonally at his head. Arthur surprised the man by stepping toward him instead of backing away. He stepped inside the arc of the handle's swing, caught the man in a twisting move at the elbow and wrist. Suddenly the club wielder was simultaneously yelling and flying through the air, head first.

The second skinhead launched a rushing attack shouting, 'you son of a bitch.' He was brought up short as Arthur met his rush with a back-kick. As the goon doubled over, Arthur followed up with a back-fist, right-cross one hand combination. He then finished the staggering attacker with a low spin-kick, just as I had earlier seen Master Kim do. The hapless biker, however, didn't have the skill to break his fall, and he landed hard, knocking himself unconscious.

"Wow, Traveler!" exclaimed Dusty. "Just like Kung-fu!"

"Hapkido, actually," I said without thinking.

They both looked at me and we all three burst out laughing.

"Shall we question them?" I asked.

"No. Let's just tie them up for the present. Dusty, see if you can find some rope."

"Won't need rope, Arthur. I brought plenty of these." He held up a bag of Bar Lock ties, the plastic ties with the self-locking loops.

"Good. Let's secure them and look for Alex before anyone else shows up," directed Arthur.

We checked out the house, but aside from a sink full of

dishes with food scraps on them, a garbage can full of empty beer cans, lots of girlie magazines and general filth, nothing was amiss. I was beginning to think that perhaps we were following a dry lead. There certainly wasn't anything occult about this place.

"Let's check the barn," suggested Arthur.

The barn didn't look all that promising. Its vertical wooden siding looked like it needed paint, but Arthur said, "Appearances can be deceiving." He continued, "For example, I wonder why the owners of this barn would go to the trouble of attempting to make this barn look run down and then go to the effort of putting on a brand new roof?" He directed my attention up.

I looked up and saw that, indeed, the roof on the apparently ramshackle structure was brand new. Further, as I eyed the weathered exterior, I found that it had been painted, like a stage set, to give the impression of age. A solid core door with a Yale lock was set just to the right of the large barn doors. These barn doors, upon examination, were not functional, having been nailed shut. The door with the lock, with a bush strategically planted before it, had fortunately been left ajar by our recently combative acquaintance. Arthur and I moved into the barn while Dusty kept watch outside. It was pitch black within, the afternoon sunlight reaching only a few feet inside.

Arthur found the light switch and flipped it on. Black light tubes along the ceiling supplied the illumination. What they revealed was bizarre. The entire barn had been given over to this temple of infamy. The walls, floor and ceiling had been painted a high gloss black. Painted in the appropriate flashing elemental colors on each of the walls was a large inverted pentagram. At the center of each of these, in white, was the name of one of the four great princes of the infernal hierarchy. From the ceiling hung a large upside-down cross. Directly below this, at the center of the large circle and swastika design was a couch-like altar. I noted that this swastika was, like that of the Third Reich, the adverse one, the opposite of the one that was a high symbol of light. Just to the east of the couch was a large sandstone block about four feet tall by four feet deep — but only two feet wide. It evidently represented the throne of "The Devil" in Tarot Key #15, the symbol of lies. As I looked closer at this 'altar,' I could see the telltale rusty stains of blood rites.

"Ugh! This place stinks with the atmosphere of the Qlippoth," remarked Arthur. "Michael, would you please bring me the suitcase containing my traveling kit from the van."

I knew that Arthur was referring to the small suitcase in which he carried certain occult paraphernalia as a sort of 'magical emergency road kit.' When I returned with the kit, Arthur pulled four things from its interior: a very ornate Pentalpha ring, which he placed upon his finger, assuming his 'mystical personality' as he did so; his Athame, in its red pentagram embossed case; and finally, a vial of clear liquid and a metal box with a dragon worked in high relief upon its lid.

He smiled as he held it up for me to see and quipped, "This is my 'Dr. Taverner box.' It contains ashes from last year's Yule log in one compartment, and consecrated salt from our last lodge meeting in the other. The glass vial contains 'holy water,' consecrated according to a special formula in use by the Fraternity."

"Let's see what we can..." just as he started this sentence, we heard a noise and froze. At first, we thought someone was knocking on the door. Then we realized someone was kicking upon the ceiling.

Dusty had also heard the noise and left his lookout at the door to join us.
 "There!" he said, pointing to a pull-down ladder in the corner that led to a trap door in the ceiling.

We quickly moved to the ladder and lowered it. I moved cautiously up the ladder, armed with the axe handle we had rescued from the tied-up-and-stored-in-the-weeds-out-back-skinheads. I pushed open the door and saw what was making the noise. Bound and gagged, wearing only her panties and bra, was a straggly haired teenage girl. She looked up at us pleadingly, like a puppy that had been beat on a regular basis. It was her foot banging on the floor that had made the knocking. The room she occupied had at one time been the hayloft. Now it looked like it served as a general storeroom for the temple.

As we hastened to untie her, Dusty went into the house

and returned with some blue jeans and a tee shirt, a couple of sizes too large, for the young lady to put on. Dusty gave her a cup of coffee.

I looked questioningly at Arthur. He shook his head and said, "No, Michael, this isn't Alex."

"I'm Renee. Do you know Alex?"

"Yes, we do," answered Arthur. "Do you know where she is?"

"If it wasn't for me, she wouldn't be in the mess she's in now," answered the girl, tears in her eyes and her Oklahoma 'twang' coming through. "I mean, I'm the one who brung her to the meetin', and I was the one who introduced her to that asshole North. If you all are friends of hers, you better get her out of this place before tonight," she finished.

"If we could find her, we would," said Dusty.

"Didn't you find her tied up in the house?"

"No, only three goons," answered Dusty.

"They must be a keepin' her up at the farm until tonight. North was really pissed at her for running away and all that telling. He was going to make her a channel or medium or something, but I heard him tell his co-chiefs that she was going to have to be punished. That's how I ended up tied up, on account I was spyin'. He said he was gonna fix me too!"

"What do you mean, fix you?" I asked.

"Tonight's May Day Eve, the night of one of their biggest parties. He means to sacrifice her and, later, me too!"

"You can't mean he's going to perform a human sacrifice?" I exclaimed.

"He's done it before. I've seen and heard. He's crazy. I'd run, but I know he'd catch me; sooner or later he'd get me back."

"You aren't just gonna give up, are you," asked Dusty?

"We're going to have to hurry," Arthur instructed us. "It's getting near sundown and I'm sure they'll want to start their festivities by mid-evening. They'll be coming back any time.

"Dusty, go use the telephone in the house and see if you can get us some back-up. Hide all of the bikes that are parked out front and leave a note attached to the front door: 'Boss - out of beer - gone to get more - be back later.'

"Meanwhile, Mike and Renee will come with me downstairs. We're going to prepare a surprise for Brother North and company. I'm going to deconsecrate or remove the protective cone of power from the circle.

Chances are, North won't notice it until it's too late."

Renee and I watched as Arthur took his Athame and banished the energies of the circle. He then went to the altar and, with time-honored formula, deconsecrated it with salt and ash, intoning the word 'Solve' in his deep, vibrating voice. He then walked counter-clockwise about the circumference of the circle, sprinkling holy water as he marched, chanting 'Procul, oh Procul este Profani.'

When he had finished, the room had lost its sinister 'Qlippothic' atmosphere and become something akin to a poorly done stage set. But the most remarkable transformation was the one that took place in Renee. It was as if she had awakened from a dream. She looked at Arthur and spoke without a trace of her accent, "You really did remove his power from this room. How do you plan to rescue Alex?"

"I plan to do it in a way that will also readjust the Cosmic balance, as far as Roman North is concerned."

"How may I help?" she asked.

"Do you think you can pretend to be tied up in the loft? I'll be hiding up there behind some of the boxes with Dr. Richardson. We'll make sure you aren't harmed, but North must believe everything is normal until the critical time. Since he is bringing Alex with him, I feel she will play the leading role tonight. She'll probably be under his glamour, just as you were until I banished the energies here, so we cannot count on her to help. Do you think you can manage that?"

"I got Alex into this, and I need to help get her out," Renee affirmed. "Besides, for the first time in months, I can taste freedom again."

"How many guards and how many celebrants will there likely be tonight?"

"Normally six guards, but you have eliminated three."

"Have we enough resources to take care of three more 'tough guys' when the time comes?" Arthur asked Dusty, who had just returned.

"More than enough select help will be stealthily advancing upon the unsuspecting three when the time arrives," quipped Dusty. "They will be in place within an hour."

"How about Roman's assistants?" Arthur asked Renee.

"One for each of the remaining three quarters, two women and one other man," she answered. "North will officiate in the East. There'll be a woman in the North and West. The other man will be in the South."

"What can you tell me about them?"

"My opinion is that only Roman is a magician. The rest are just there to contribute their energy and fill the roles.

I've only seen two of these events, though, and I was in a daze all that time."

An hour and a half passed until we finally heard the motorcycles approaching. Arthur and I watched from the window in the loft as three bikers arrived with a black Mercedes carrying five people. One of the people fit North's description, and beside him was an attractive teenage girl. North started first to call for his missing guards. He then saw the note and cursed in a loud voice. He spoke to the other guards, who took up positions to the front and rear of the barn and on the front porch of the house.

Renee had taken her place and feigned unconsciousness just as the trap door opened and one of the women looked in on her. The ruse worked, for the woman called down the ladder to North that everything was as it should be.

Appearances can be deceiving. I chuckled silently. As I watched from the window, I could see each of the guards being 'taken out' by Dusty and his fellow bikers. Soon, Dusty and friends were standing in the shadows, taking the place of the guards, while North's men joined the three earlier casualties in the weeds.

Arthur and I were watching through a peephole in the trap door as North and his three assistants began to disrobe. If it had not been for my knowledge that North had committed murder more than once, and had tortured animals and people in service to his foul quest for power, I would have laughed out loud. North's flabby body with his potbelly and spindly legs was not exactly the physique that inspired awe. The two women and the other man who were to be his co-workers were no better. The other man was probably in his sixties, and reminded me of a scarecrow, as did one of the others. The remaining woman was in her mid-forties and rather attractive, in a mannish sort of way. The three assistants wore black robes of a silken material with the hood of their robe drawn forward over their heads. North wore a robe of bright crimson, and upon his head he placed an iron circlet emblazoned in front with an inverted pentagram, the symbol of the subjugation of the human spirit.

I marveled at the transformation that occurred. Before my very eyes Roman North became the embodiment of an evil being, an unclean, sacrificial priest ready to offer blood to appease his dark gods. These gods were named on the walls about his temple. Would they come in answer to his summons, in response to his offering, to claim the life essence of the young girl who stood in a trance-like stupor, oblivious to her peril?

The younger woman had ignited a brazier and was throwing incense upon the hot coals. As clouds of smoke billowed up with its noxious fumes, I could see North circumambulating the four quarters. He stopped before each of the up-side-down stars upon the walls and chanted his call in a horse, guttural language that I didn't recognize. The vibrations seemed to penetrate to the core of my soul, chilling and repelling my spirit. I started to shake, and perhaps would have collapsed if Arthur had not put his hand upon my shoulder. I tore my attention away from the macabre drama unfolding on the floor below me to an even more fabulous vision.

While I had been observing all that was going on below, Arthur had opened his traveling kit and effected a marvelous transformation in himself. Arthur Alexander stood before me robed in his august office as Chief of The Council of the Pentalpha, the visible representative of the Third Order, he who strides the abyss, linking the visible with the invisible, the Steward, servant of the Light! As I looked at him, tall in his pure white robe and crimson and gold floor length cape, I saw in him the office of Guardian of the Mysteries that stretched back to the Temple of Atlantis. Upon his breast was the heavy gold Lamen of the Pentalpha. He was crowned with the golden crown of the four pentagrams. In his right hand he held the flaming sword of Geburah.

I don't know how long I would have stood and stared if he had not broken the spell by speaking. "Michael, Renee, it is time we rewrote the script for the drama unfolding below. Michael, open the trap door."

Renee and I, still quite in awe of the figure before us, could feel the power crackling about him. I perceived a visible aura of power, and a wavering in the appearance of my friend, intermittently superimposed by another image of an ancient and potent priest-king.

We lifted the trap door back and Arthur descended,

while Renee and I watched from the opening. North had persuaded Alex, nude and completely oblivious to what was going on around her, to lie down upon the couch. Brandishing a knife with a curved blade, North began an invocation to his obscene gods, beings of the pit, of the Qlippoth. With a strange sensitivity that I had experienced before in situations of high psychic energy, I could see horrible forms gather in the thick smoke pouring from the brazier. Malignant, leering countenances, faces with horns and hands with talons were reaching for that young victim upon the altar. Sensing their nearness, exalting in this borrowed power, his eyes shining manically, North raised his arms high, preparing to bring the knife down, and shouted: "Give us your favor, oh princes of the dark hierarchies. Behold! We bring you a pure sacrifice without blemish!"

At this moment, Arthur, resplendent in his robes and crown, holding aloft his flaming magical sword of Justice, sang forth in a clear ringing voice the clarion call of 'The Adoration,' that Gnostic invocation of the Light that had been used by Adepts and Initiates of the right-hand Path of the Divine Mysteries for untold ages:

> "Holy Art Thou! Oh Lord of the Universe!
> Holy Art Thou, Whom Nature hath not formed!
> Holy Art Thou, Oh Vast and Mighty One!
> Lord of the Light, and of the Darkness."

One of the priestesses turned and, seeing Arthur, shrieked, "An Adept of Light is amongst us! Flee!"

With that, she and the other three stampeded through the door, only to be met by Dusty and his companions.

North, turning after them, yelled, "Fools, why do you run? We are invincible in our dedicated circle!" Facing Arthur, he pointed his knife and called out, "Oh, princes of the descending steps of the Qlippoth! Drive forth this invading contagion, show forth your power!"

Arthur assumed a stance with legs wide apart and arms held straight out to each side. As the cloud creatures started towards him, he answered the challenge: "Let the Light from the Divine Crown descend!" He then intoned the potent 'Pentagrammaton,' or holy name of five letters. As he did, a flaming pentagram seemed to superimpose itself upon his figure. The very air around him crackled and scintillated with power.

The horned and taloned ones in the clouds of incense recoiled from that symbol as if acid had been thrown at them. They howled their impotent fury as they sought some target upon which to vent their rage. One of the demons sought to reach Alex, but a bolt of lightning-like energy shot forth from Arthur's flaming sword and vaporized him, leaving only a mournful wail as he was cast back into the pit from which he came. The others turned their frustration upon North, who dropped his knife and stood rigid, shaking as if high voltage electricity coursed through him.

In an instant, all was silent. It was over. North collapsed, still rigid in death, the power he had sought to direct for the ruin and enslavement of others exacting a terrible revenge against him as it rebounded. The other three co-workers did not escape either. We found them curled into a catatonic fetal position, each one having retreated somewhere deep within the subconscious mind as the Qlippothic beings had pursued them.

* * * * *

With the sunrise we gathered together in 'The Lady' in Stillwater. Alex and Renee enjoyed a reunion. Keith was thankful that his daughter had no memory of last night, and little memory of what had occurred since her abduction. The barn had caught fire from the brazier being knocked over by one of North's fleeing assistants, and had burned to the ground, along with the body of Roman North.

"Burning is the traditional method of disposing of a sorcerer's body," Arthur said philosophically.

After receiving warnings from Dusty's buddies, the skinhead guards had fled, fearing police involvement. Having seen what had happened to their former boss, they were probably on the far side of Amarillo by now, on their way west, the fear of God contributing to their speed.

The authorities had received an anonymous tip that the fire, the charred corpse and three catatonics were the result of a bad batch of acid and trips gone awry. There was much truth in that.

120

Even with the fantastic events of the previous night still on our minds, the mood of the group of friends sitting around the bookstore was almost festive. We had been through the dark night of the soul together and had emerged safely on the other side.

It was agreed that Alex would be attending school on the outskirts of Los Angeles this coming fall, and staying with her godfather until her father was able to relocate to Riverside. She turned to Arthur and grasped both of his hands, "Oh Uncle Arthur, I knew you'd come for me!"

Arthur smiled and said fondly, "Of course! You called to me, didn't you?"

DRUMS IN THE NIGHT

Have you ever considered the phenomenon known as 'coincidence'? This is the word by which materialists and skeptics in every country explain away, dismiss, or otherwise try to discount anything that does not fit into their preconceived image of the Cosmos. Someone once said that if any other area of study besides occultism and metaphysics had the abundant testimony of evidence supporting it, it would have been accepted as fact. But with the study of the hidden powers and laws of the universe and the mind, many orthodox scientists simply choose to ignore the testimony of nature. At any rate, as Einstein said, "Imagination is more important than intelligence."

So it was with some surprise that I viewed Dr. Arthur Alexander's casual comment to me as we walked across campus from the faculty center to one of the libraries. He asked me if I wanted to hear about a coincidence that had occurred that morning. Of course I did!

"Just this morning I was lecturing about the worldwide traditions concerning ghosts and haunting, and this afternoon I received a phone call from Toronto requesting that I exorcise a haunted house."

"Toronto, Canada? Was it a prank?"

"Yes, Canada, and no, they were very serious. You

remember that house your cousin Roderick was remodeling in England when he found the secret rooms in the basement? Well, the owner of that house has some rather wealthy friends, society people; you know the type. They are always attending this function or that and getting their pictures in the papers. They go to dinners and dances and say they're raising money for a good cause."

We both chuckled appreciatively at his satiric description.

"This couple wanted to get back to nature; provided, of course, that nature included a fully stocked bar, a large fire place, television, satellite disk, VCR, a spa and king size beds. They purchased some land up in the woods northeast of Toronto, near a small town called Peterborough, and had a custom cabin built according to specifications."

"Nice to be rich," I commented wryly.

"But a very curious turn of events took place on the night before they were to throw their cabin-warming party. Around midnight they heard the rushing of wind through the trees."

"Isn't that one of the advantages of having a place in the woods? To have enough quiet to hear the breeze in the trees?"

"That would be fine, except for three things. One, this is

no breeze. It sounded like a tornado. Two, they only hear it in the guest bedroom on the east side of the house. If they go outside or into another room, it is still – no wind – nada."

"Could someone be playing tricks?" I suggested.

"On themselves? No. I don't see any motive for that. Besides, you haven't heard number three yet. The evening of the party was a full moon, and in the bright moonlight they distinctly saw a young girl, a maiden, if you will, her hair blowing in the wind, dressed like an Indian."

"There's something more to that, I'm sure?" I asked skeptically.

"Well, I supposed so, if you take into consideration the fact that this young Indian maiden was walking in the air."

"I'm starting to get the idea," I replied.

"Additionally, there is a wolf seen at the dark of the moon. It is always seen to be running through flames, where no fire can possibly be. And, oh yes, one more thing…"

"You mean there's more?"

"There is the sound of drums; drums in the night. They can't get a decent night's sleep because of the sound of

Indian tom-toms. It goes on for hours at a time on some nights."

"Isn't it unusual to have a haunted house built to order? Doesn't someone usually have to be killed in it, or something like that? You know, been in the family for generations, etc."

"That's what sparked my interest," answered Arthur. "A newly built house seeming to have inherited some rather unique spooks."

"How are the owners taking it?"

"At first they thought it would entertain their guests, but they found out that the weirdness of the phenomena began to be attached to themselves by their jet-set friends. Rather like having a contagious disease. This, of course, could not be tolerated. To be a witness to paranormal phenomena is one thing, but to have your so-called friends think you are somehow connected and thereby risk social stigma is an entirely different case altogether!"

"So they want you to come up and chase the spooks out?"

"That's about the size of it," Arthur answered dryly. "I wouldn't bother, except for one or two things."

"What things?" I asked, taking the bait.

"The uniqueness of the apparitions, for one. If the haunts were the normal etheric shades, shaking chains, I would not have spared them a second thought. There has got to be an interesting story connected with these phenomena. The second reason, and the most important to me, was the fact that I had a dream last week. In the dream, I was visited by my Third Order contact and an old Indian shaman, or medicine man. There were asking for my help. If that wasn't 'coincidental' enough, they were accompanied by two others: a young Indian maiden with blowing hair, and what appeared to be a large gray wolf – walking through flames."

I let out a long low whistle, and he looked at me knowingly.

"When do we leave for Toronto?" I asked.

"I've booked us tickets on United to arrive just before the full moon."

* * * * *

As we passed through Customs, the smiling face of a slightly built, white-bearded man in his fifties met us. In short order, I was introduced to another of Arthur's fellow travelers, Mr. Nathan Rierdon, the Preceptor for the Order in Canada. We were escorted to a waiting car driven by one of Nathan's Sorors, Sharon McDonnell. Sharon was an attractive blond in her mid-thirties. She had that trick of looking at you without looking at you. That is, she would appear to be focusing, at times, just

127

to either side and a little behind you. My experiences with Arthur had taught me that this was a technique used by initiates when they wished to view someone's aura. When Arthur mentioned that she was one of the Guardians of the local Temple, I was impressed that she had achieved this at such a young age.

On the way up the road towards Peterborough, I was prepared to eavesdrop on the conversation of these three initiates, hoping to learn more about this amazing fraternity that had begun to hold such a fascination for me. Imagine my frustration when the conversation turned toward major league baseball! Our hosts took turns giving us a good-natured ribbing about the fact that Toronto was the home of the World Champion Blue-Jays, who had now won the World Series two years in a row. Arthur and I resorted to the defense that, even in baseball, miracles still happen.

As we neared our destination, I looked out of the car window at the rolling hills with their stands of birch trees. I could easily imagine the Indian maiden walking through the woods with her dog. On impulse, I turned toward Nathan and asked, "Nathan, I imagine there must have been many tribes of Native Americans here at one time. Am I right?"

"Oh, yes," he replied. "There are, in fact, some Indian burial grounds not far from Peterborough. The Indian population was quite extensive, but they still managed to live in harmony with the environment. It's a pity we Anglos haven't learned that lesson yet. Instead, we have air pollution, deforestation, and acid rain."

"What happened to the Indians?" I asked.

"Oh, mostly they were just pushed out. Bows and arrows don't compete well with guns and powder. Besides, when the Europeans came to these lands, they brought their diseases with them. Some tribes, even their names forgotten now, were simply wiped out in a very short time because of their lack of immunity."

I fell back in my seat, daydreaming on what it must have been like here before the coming of the Europeans. I must have dozed off, for the next thing I became aware of was Sharon's hand on my shoulder, and her voice telling me we had arrived. I sat up and looked out the car window. We had pulled up in front of a large, two-story house built from cedar boards, laid in a wedge or herringbone design. Across the front on the second story ran a sundeck, the garage being beneath this. To the right of the "cabin" I could see the satellite reception dish.

The others were already carrying their luggage up the stairway that was just to the left of the deck. I got out, stretched, and took a deep breath. The smell of the trees, the earth, and the nearby lake – everything blended together to create a sense of vitality and aliveness. It made every sense tingle with a simple joy. If I hadn't been aware that this site was haunted, I would have named it the perfect retreat. Still, I have to admit to a certain feeling of anticipation when I gazed at the upstairs windows of the cabin, like a small boy fantasizing about what lies within that oversized package beneath the Christmas tree. My interest had become more and more heightened in the areas of the mystical, esoteric, and paranormal the longer my association with Arthur Alexander continued. Whatever innate fear I might have had in regards to this haunted house had been replaced by the acquired fascination this prospect now held for me. I had glimpsed the workings of the hidden side of life, and now its call was sounding in my soul. Deep called to deep, and the seeker responded with enthusiasm.

As I mounted the stairs, suitcase in hand, Warren Greystone, the unhappy owner of the cabin, greeted me. He looked to be in his late forties, dark hair with a touch of gray at the temples. He favored me with a picture-perfect smile and said:

"Welcome to Falcon crest, Dr. Richardson! Let me show you to your bedroom. The others have already started to settle in and freshen up. Dr. Alexander suggested that we all gather in the fireplace room so I can brief you before I leave."

"You're not staying, then?" I asked in surprise.

"No. I, ah, how shall I put it?" he began. "I believe it would be better for me to come back after the problem has been taken care of."

Somehow I got the distinct impression that he viewed

the "problem" as others might view a termite infestation, and we were the exterminators, arriving to tent the house.

"Here is your room, Dr. Richardson," our host said as he opened the door to a bedroom with a large sliding glass door opening out onto the deck.

"Which direction is this deck facing?" I asked.

"That's the east," he answered. "You'll probably wake up to the morning sun shining through the windows."

"This is the east bedroom, then." I murmured, more to myself than to him.

"I beg your pardon?"

"Oh, nothing. This is a beautiful place."

"Yes. We are, of course, very disappointed with the way this has developed. In fact, we have just about decided to place this site on the market and buy a place near Edinburgh. There is so much more tradition in Great Britain, you know. Nothing of ancient culture or civilization around here exists. There were only Indians here, and they had little to offer anyone of culture."

"Perhaps it is just a 'type' question," I suggested.

"I beg your pardon?" he sounded confused.

"Type. You know, some people have more of an affinity with early American furniture, and some gravitate toward Contemporary Danish. It's the same for different cultures, I would think," I tried to explain. "You seem to be an Anglophile, while others are very passionate about Native American traditions. Some people have suggested that the root of these likes and dislikes lie in past lives."

"You believe in reincarnation?" asked Mr. Greystone incredulously.

"Yes, sir, I do," I confessed. "I've witnessed some things that have convinced me of its validity. After all, the numbers of people who believe in reincarnation far out-number the people who don't. Almost every major religion, including Christianity, support it, or at least, supported it at one time."

"Certainly," he commented. "It just seems sort of exotic. But I'd forgotten – you're a professor of comparative religions, aren't you?" He smiled, obviously satisfied that he'd discovered how an apparently civilized, if not too bright, man such as myself could entertain the notion, or even profess to believe in such a superstitious theory as rebirth. I was content to let the conversation turn to other subjects as I mused over the stories I had heard recently about the east bedroom.

As agreed, we gathered in the room on the opposite side of the large cabin from my quarters, called "the fireplace room," which was dominated by a large, natural rock fireplace with a thick oak plank mantel. The obligatory moose-head trophy above the mantel presided over a well-appointed bar, big screen TV, and assorted arcade games. Obviously, entertainment was the keynote for this part of the domicile. Our host poured each of us refreshment as we settled down onto the expensive couch and easy chairs.

"I'll come right to the point," he began, in what I assumed was the no-nonsense-bottom-line voice he used in dealing with employees and others with whom he had contracted services. "I've spent a lot of money on this building, and now I can't use it because of this damnable phenomenon that some idiotic people say are spooks. I only know one thing: This is my property. I didn't invite these things here, and I won't have them gatecrashing. I've been told that you people can take care of the problem. That's what I'm after. I'm not interested in your philosophy. I'd rather not know your methods. I'm only interested in results.

"So, I'm going to leave you folks to it. I'd just be in your way, so I'm going back to Toronto." He handed me a slip of paper. "If you really need me, here's my hotel. Otherwise, I'll expect to hear from you Monday, three days from now. I'll take my leave now, unless you have any questions."

Within ten minutes, Mr. Greystone had gone. Arthur spoke up, looking at each of us. "Has anyone noticed the extreme sensation of elemental vitality that this place exudes?"

"I thought it was just my imagination," I answered, with my mouth dropping open.

"Oh no, Michael," affirmed Sharon. "I noticed it also, as soon as I stepped from the car. It's like a tonic. A weekend around this place would be better than a whole bottle of vitamins."

"Notice also that this building is built on what, in the near-East, is called a 'tell,'" continued Arthur.

"A tell?" questioned Nathan. "Then you think this is not the first structure to be built upon this site? That there is possibly an archeological connection to the phenomena?"

"Most likely. I suggest we rest and then reconvene back here at about four. We'll cast a circle of protection, and then I'm going out on the Astral, to the invisible temple, to see what I can find out from my Fratres et Sorores there. Michael, would you care to come along?"

I did a visible double take as the implication of his words began to dawn on me. "You want me to accompany you onto the Astral? Can that be done? I mean, I thought it was your own subconsciousness. I didn't think you could actually share a journey."

Arthur smiled and nodded once. "If that were true, Michael, then astral workings would be totally subjective and lacking in objective existence. But initiates have been shown the reality of the inner planes. Dion Fortune once wrote that 'what I imagine is subjective, but what we both imagine becomes objective.' This is the difference between a path working for initiates, and the watered-down guided meditations found in many published books. When we enter the inner worlds via a specific symbolic portal, we will find ourselves in essentially the same symbolic environment that any other initiate, using the gateway, would experience. Thus, we have certain 'locations' that have been built up for centuries, even millennia, by both those working on the earth plane of consciousness, and those inner partners with whom we work. These have an existence, a reality that is independent and more lasting than the changing conditions of the physical plane. Many have described these as parallel universes, but in reality, they are simply different dimensions of this one."

"But I have no experience to know how to get to that dimension or, probably more important to me, how to get back!"

"Oh, you'd be in secure hands, Michael," chuckled Nathan. "Better or more experienced ones would be hard to find, at least on this side of the Abyss, right Sharon?"

"I'll take you through the gate," Arthur reassured me. "In fact, since you are not yet an initiate, you would be turned back by the guardian before you reached the Hall of the Archives."

My attention was sparked when I heard the words, "not yet an initiate." My mind put special emphasis on the word, 'yet,' which seemed to hold the promise that someday I might achieve admission to the group of travelers I had so grown to admire.

 "Ok, I'm game," I answered.

We had a light repast from the ample provisions of the kitchen, and Nathan, Sharon and Arthur turned in early. I was much too excited to sleep however, so I turned on the television, not expecting to find anything worth watching. As I was channel surfing, I happened upon an old rerun of "Thriller," hosted by Boris Karloff. This episode, entitled "Dark legacy," was about a second-rate magician who had inherited his uncle's magic book, and his pet demon, Astroreth. It made a point of the danger of meddling with unseen power. It was a little after eleven when I finally made my way to the east bedroom and threw myself, still fully clothed, across the bed.

I don't know how long I had been asleep when I entered into a sort of half dream. The rushing of the breeze through the trees and then the sound of drums – drums in the night, had heralded her coming. I could see her clearly in the moonlight. She was about five feet two inches tall with brown flowing hair, tossed by the wind. She was dressed in the buckskins and furs of the northern Indian tribes. I thought she was one of the most beautiful women I had ever seen. She had that unearthly, ethereal, exotic quality that mesmerizes men. As I looked into her eyes, I was startled to see tears pouring down her cheeks. She held her arms out to me, imploringly. Her voice echoed plaintively in my ears, "Help us. Please!"

I awoke and found that I was standing before the sliding glass doors, gazing at the moonlit woods below. She had pleaded with me for help. I felt that I would do anything to help her, but I checked the lock on the doors carefully before I returned to bed. I had no wish to pursue her off the second story balcony.

Shortly before four that morning I freshened up and went to join the others in the fireplace room. The furniture had been cleared from the middle of the room, except for two chairs facing each other in the center. Sharon placed a tall glass votive candle holder in each of the four cardinal directions: a yellow one in the east, red in the south, blue in the west, and a dark indigo one in the north. Arthur placed his red leather case with the gold pentagram inscribed upon its lid upon the floor beside the couch. He opened it and took from it his 'krill,' or dagger with the wavy blade. Sharon produced a silver goblet and proceeded to fill it from a bottle of water she had brought. Simultaneously, Nathan was busy over a censer and incense boat, lighting the charcoal and spooning frankincense into the thurible. I was given some salt upon a platter and told to be prepared to sprinkle a little in a circular pattern about the room when instructed to do so. Finally, Arthur spread two sleeping bags upon the floor in the space between the facing chairs. He then directed Nathan to dim the lights, and pronounced all was prepared for the erection of the Astral Fortress that would safeguard us as we went forth as 'flying souls' upon the Astral Plane, and provide us with a safe harbor in this psychically uncertain environment.

Arthur directed us to stand in the four quarters of the room, equal distances from each other and the furniture in the center of the cleared space. Arthur stood in the east, Nathan in the south, Sharon in the west, and I occupied the north. Arthur began with the ancient Gnostic invocation of praise known as the "Adoration":

"Holy art Thou, Lord of the Universe.
Holy art Thou, Whom Nature hath not formed.
Holy art Thou, oh Vast and Mighty One.
Lord of the Light, and of the Darkness."

He then proceeded to circumambulate the rest of the open space, and us pausing at each of the quarters to draw in the air with his dagger certain seals. At each of these, he would chant strange words in his sonorous voice. I received the vague psychic impression that these words were hurled forth to the far corners of the universe. The image sprang into my mind of four towers, guarded by immense and powerful archangelic presences that answered my friend's call.

As I mused over these impressions, Arthur gently cued me to start in the north and retrace his path, sprinkling the blessed salt about the circle. I seemed to see the salt sparkle as it flew from my fingertips to the floor.

As I took my place back in the north, Sharon began to pace the circle, starting in the west, sprinkling water as she went. She called forth in a ringing voice certain passages, which I recognized were taken from "The Chaldean Oracles":

"And the priest purified with the lustral waters."

 I began to see, flickering in and out of my perception, a softly glowing band of bluish-white light following the path that we had laid down. I knew by this that psychic and astral stresses were being established around us, and that this construction on the subtle etheric plane is what would constitute our protection.

Nathan concluded the warding by circumambulating with the smoking censor, clouds of the sweet-smelling frankincense swirling and curling from the swinging brass vessel.

As Nathan finished, Arthur directed each of us to place our respective elements behind us on the perimeter of the circle. We then stepped forward and joined hands, each joining our down-facing right palm with the other's up-facing left palm. I could feel a tingling similar to what I had experienced playing with low voltage batteries as a boy, or the feeling of the blood returning to a limb that has 'gone to sleep.'

Arthur then spoke, looking at each of us in turn. "We

are gathered in this sacred space, between the worlds, in a moment outside of time, beyond the tumbling hourglass. For we are Initiates, and we have gathered as our Fratres and Sorores have done down through the ages, from the misty times of the beginnings. We are gathered together and – we – are – One! In the Name of the Adonai, the Lord, may all the Nations be blessed."

As these words echoed in the room, I felt the energy in the room increase, find its balance, and stabilize into a firm supporting foundation. I was then instructed to lie down upon one of the sleeping bags with my left ankle crossed over my right. Sharon suggested that I place the interlaced fingers of both hands over my solar plexus, explaining that this would regulate and seal the flow of the currents in my etheric body.

As she was instructing me, I noticed that Arthur had quietly and gracefully assumed an identical posture upon the other sleeping bag. Nathan then instructed us to begin a deep, rhythmic breathing pattern. I noticed that both he and Sharon synchronized their breathing to ours. When he judged me to be sufficiently relaxed, Nathan leaned forward and with the first two fingers and thumb of his right hand, began to tap a strange, syncopated beat lightly upon the area between my eyebrows. The effect of this light tapping was both curious and immediate. I became aware of an urge to sneeze, but instead of working into a full-blown "ah-choo," it seemed to go up and in.

A gauzy veil came across my vision, and when I closed

my eyes, I saw a softly glowing light just above the spot
Nathan was drumming. Finally, I heard a loud snap, and
I found myself staring at the ceiling, which was about
six inches in front of my face. I might have panicked if I
hadn't felt the steadying hand of Arthur upon my
shoulder. I was beside him at ceiling height. We turned
now, looking down at our circle where Nathan and
Sharon were seated in their chairs with our bodies lying
on the sleeping bags between them. If ever I needed
evidence that I was not my body, or for the immortality
of the soul, that evidence now had been provided. I was
now a flying soul, one who could step forth from the
vehicle of flesh into the vehicle of light. True, this had
only been possible under the guidance of my friend;
still, the experience was exhilarating and liberating.

I noticed the triple circle glowing about us, with
Arthur's pentagrams coldly and steadily flowing about
our group. I noted something else. Dimly visible, like a
double exposure with the images badly faded, I could
discern the outline of an ancient, rough stone circle
surrounding the house. At the cardinal points of this
circle was a trilithonic gateway made of two large
uprights with a third stone laid across their tops. These
gateways appeared to be approximately five feet wide
by eight feet tall. Pointing to the stones, I asked Arthur,
"Where did those come from? They weren't there when
we were in our bodies."

"They are the shadows of a structure that existed there
long ago. They must have been centers for a very great
power to have subsisted for so long.

"Come," he said, placing a hand upon my shoulder, "we must construct and pass through a gate of our own."

We turned and I saw a large stone pylon gateway form. Arthur stepped forward and traced a symbol before this portal. Then, gesturing for me to follow, he walked through the door and vanished. Seeing no other course but to follow, I too passed between those ancient stones and found myself standing beside a smiling Arthur in a scene from another time and another place.

We stood upon a grassy knoll overlooking a formal maze planted with rose bushes of various kinds. On the other side of the garden rose a majestic pyramid-like temple. Here and there I saw small groups and couples of white robed people walking, talking, or reading from scrolls. I had never been in surroundings so peaceful and conducive to inner reflection. When I mentioned this to Arthur, he smiled and answered, "The atmosphere of a temple's precincts mirror the state of mind of its initiates. This temple is supported by adepts who indeed are the embodiment of the most lofty states of consciousness, for this is the home of the Invisible Order, and that mountain that backs that pyramid is known as the 'Mystical Mountain of Illumination.'"

I turned and saw an olive-skinned man in a white robe. He had very full, black hair which was combed straight back. He wore what in earlier days would have been called a van dyke beard. What impressed me more than any other feature was the luminous quality of his eyes.

They radiated an almost visible power. "Michael," Arthur said, smiling, "may I formally present to you our Frater Franciscus Christian Rakoczy, the Count de Saint Germain."

I started to go down on my knees before this obviously spiritually advanced person, but he stopped me, stating, "No, Michael, there is no reason to kneel before me! I'm a man, just like you. True, I may have traveled a few more roads than you, but that just gave me the opportunity to make a few more mistakes, and perhaps to benefit from their lessons." He and Arthur shared a laugh at that, but I was still too awed by his presence.

"Extremely Honored Frater," Arthur addressed the bearded man, "you know why we have come to the Temple. We all sense that this affair we have become involved in bears a greater design than what is apparent on the surface of these events."

"This is true," answered Rakoczy. "This place where your circle now stands is a place most sacred and most critical to all of us. I have requested our Frater Red Bird to explain more fully." Rakoczy gestured to a man dressed in the garments of a Native American Shaman who was approaching us.

Red Bird greeted us and slowly began to reveal to us the story of the sacred grove and circle. He explained how the planet Earth possessed an etheric body, just like a human being. Just as the human etheric body had great energy vortexes known as charkas, so did the body of the Mother Earth. This place where Mr. Greystone has built his vacation cabin is the physical location that correlated with one of these centers. This center was unique in that it is one of the very few places where the gateways for the energy exchange of all four of the ancient elements, fire, earth, air and water, flowed from the inner worlds to the outer and back. For my sake, I'm sure; Red Bird explained that these elements shouldn't be thought of as ordinary fire, earth, air and water, but as potent forms of vital life energy critical to the health and balance of Nature and the Earth Herself. This sacred center had been placed under the guardianship of a certain tribe of indigenous people into which Red Bird had incarnated for several lifetimes as a shaman or priest. They had built a stone circle, surrounded by a grove of living trees. The shamans of this tribe had used this site as a ceremonial temple, and through their esoteric knowledge of the inner worlds, maintained the subtle link between humanity and the soul of nature that was vital to the continued harmony and balance in our world.

All things went well until, about three hundred years ago, the Europeans came to this land seeking a new home to hunt, farm, and eventually to settle. Unfortunately, they also brought measles. Having had no exposure and so no immunity to the disease, the entire tribe had been wiped out within six months. With the passing of this people from physical existence, the guardianship of the balance was lost. Slowly at first, but gaining momentum, this breaking of the subtle inner bond has become more visible to us in the form of mass scale pollution of the air and water. Now there are holes in the ozone layer, acid rain, and over population.

"Soon," Red Bird said gravely, "the sun will rise no more. Even though all of these signs can be attributed to outer causes, we of the Mysteries know that this is only an appearance. In truth, nothing ever occurs that does not have an inner cause. Truly, my brothers, the link is not being maintained. With every passing year, the balance is further disturbed. Soon, it will be impossible to restore it. Soon the Mother will no longer be able to support life."

"What must we do, my brother?" asked Arthur.

"We must reestablish the Guardianship of the Balance. Dedicated ones must be found to maintain the concourse."

"So mote it be," said Arthur nodding to Red Bird and Rakoczy.

So mote it be – so mote it be – The phrase echoed in my mind as I awoke from my trance to find Nathan and Sharon smiling down at me. Sharon offered me a cup of steaming hot cocoa, identical to the one I saw Arthur sipping. I was glad to have it, for I was chilled to the bone. Arthur recounted everything that had transpired at the Astral Temple to our Canadian Frater and Soror.

"No wonder this place has such a feel of vitality," Sharon commented.

"Before we banish this circle," Arthur stated, "we have a pledge to fulfill."

Following Arthur, we faced first the east and then the south, west and finally the north. He spoke, and we repeated with him, that ancient esoteric set of four invocations known as the "Prayers of the Elementals." It was both fulfilling and emotionally cathartic for me. As we completed the prayers at each quarter, we were thanked on the subtle level. In the east, by the Indian maiden: from the south, a young Indian warrior accompanied by a gray wolf walking through flames; in the west, a gray-haired, smiling Indian woman offering us a drink; and in the North, by our friend, Red Bird.

With a great sense of fulfillment and a sense of deep communion, we banished the circle and returned the room to its everyday appearance. We sat in the easy chairs before the fire discussing the implications of the evening's events.

"What are you going to tell Greystone?" asked Nathan.

"I'm going to admit complete failure," answered Arthur.

"You're going to do what?" I exclaimed.

"I'm going to tell Mr. Warren Greystone," (with a shrug of his shoulders and palms held up in a gesture that seemed to say 'what else can I do?') "That these spooks are extraordinarily powerful and I have been totally unsuccessful in chasing them away, and that I am sure anyone else would be equally unsuccessful."

"Is that true?" I asked.

"Of course it is!" Arthur responded. "These spooks are the embodiment of the vital forces of Nature. They mirror the consciousness of the elements. Their form, their images, veil the persons known as 'the Kings.' Even though their forms manifest at this particular power center differently from the traditional images that we use in the Fraternity, the essence is the same, and just as powerful. After all, these intelligences are primarily on the 'mind' side of consciousness. It is our subconsciousness that provides their garments, just as it does for dreams."

"You mean that lovely Indian maiden was in reality a King? I thought she liked me," I feigned hurt feelings.

"Your reception by the Elemental Potencies was very friendly, very acknowledging," Sharon answered.

"Yes, indeed," Arthur added. "That is very unusual for a non-initiate to experience. I believe we would have to look to your past lives to explain this link you obviously hold with the Elemental Kingdoms."

"I look forward to that," I answered.

Arthur said nothing, but I thought I caught a quick smiling glance exchanged between Sharon and Nathan.

One month later, Rabbi Bergman, my fiancé, Linda, and I were enjoying a brandy after a fine dinner with Arthur at his hacienda-style home. Arthur was filling the group in on the broad details of the story to a rapt audience. I, of course, was sutably modest in respect to the shared glory as a co-hero in this latest adventure.

"Well, tell us," Linda questioned, "what did Mr. Greystone say when you told him that his problem had not been solved?"

"Actually, I think he was relieved," Arthur responded. "He really wanted that place in Edinburgh and was more than looking for an excuse to 'get out from under' the place in Peterborough. By some coincidence, he had an offer from a folklore society to take the place off his hands at a fair price."

"A folklore society?" asked Linda.

"Well, actually it was a neo-pagan organization called the "Champions of the Earth Mother.""

"I think you've misled all of us," commented the Rabbi.

"How so," asked Arthur, raising his eyebrows?

"You told us that you failed in your exorcism."

"Yes. And...?" asked Arthur.

"I think you were very successful," said Bergman.

"Really?" Arthur said with a knowing smile.

"Yes. You did an admirable job of exorcising the place of those snobs, the Greystones," finished the Rabbi.

THE JEWEL OF KHEM

Marilyn awoke to the sound of a scream repeated again and again, very near. The sounds froze her twenty two year old body into immobility. It took her a few seconds before she realized that it was her screams. The door crashed opened, spilling the light of the hallway across the rumpled and twisted blankets surrounding her form, as she stood like a fence post, upright on her bed. Phillip, her brother, rushed into the room looking only slightly less disheveled in his striped pajamas. He grabbed his sister and started crooning and rocking her in his arms. Her screams died away to his relief but his anxiety returned a hundred fold when he looked at Marilyn's face. For her eyes stared back at him in a fixed, uncomprehending stare. She looked straight at and fixedly through him. He could tell she didn't see him or anything else. Her mind was locked away, far away from everything around her, somewhere else, another place, perhaps another time.

*   *   *   *   *

One year ago to the day –

The movements resembled a ballet, a beautiful landscape of movement, color, light and sound. Attractive young ladies and gentlemen dressed in flowing robes moved amidst fragrant, swirling clouds of sweet incense. Dimly flickering candlelight illuminated their bodies as they circled. The sound of their light voices were lifted in lilting prayers and invocations. The outward form of the ceremony was indeed impressive. Its flavor was light, airy, definitely in keeping with the New Age philosophy of its participants. All young, either college students or those just graduated. All members of a former university, student- interest group organized to study and explore alternative religious approaches. Also its purpose was to counteract the suppressive, stifling influence of their fellow students who had freely organized into right-wing fundamentalist coalitions.

But tonight the ceremony was charged. The mood, the atmosphere was like a violin string being tuned higher and higher. The tension floated, almost tangibly visible, like the incense smoke floating around the consecrated circle. Tonight the coven was exploring lands unknown, territory alien to them.

Up to this time, they had reserved their questings to that of experimenting with Solar and Fire Festivals – the eight great sabbats of the year. These, they had taken mostly from Stewart and Janet Ferrar's books and modified them slightly to reflect their "New Age" emphasis.

But a chance encounter with a more ancient tradition, that of the "Dark Mirror" or shewstone had deflected them onto a new path.

Marilyn had been the President and moving power behind the university club. Disillusioned by the orthodoxy's cold dogma, lack of experiential activities and the relegation of women to second-class citizenship she and the others had elected to eagerly seek out the roots of the feminine in those paths that honored the Great Mother. So, with the flood of beginning texts purporting to tell you "all you need to know," that hit the market in support of the New Age movement, it was a natural permutation for them to move to Neo-paganism. And when the group decided to stay together after graduation, Marilyn had formed them into the "Children of the Moon" coven.

They shared their avid passion for reading of books on Wicca, Paganism and New Age. These selections could be now easily found at Barnes and Noble, Borders or B. Dalton's bookstores.

But Marilyn also prowled the smaller stores in search of hard to find, out of print treasures. And, being so close to a famous city like Salem she couldn't resist exploring its wide variety of unique bookstores and supply shops.

It was in one of these shops, a small, very specialized store located on an obscure, back street that attracted her attention one rainy afternoon. As Marilyn was walking down the street, huddled beneath her brightly colored umbrella, looking down trying to avoid the puddles on the pavement that she noted some arcane symbols that had been painted on the sidewalk in front of an entrance. Perhaps it was these devices with their mystical, summoning spell or maybe it was just her curiosity and desire to seek shelter from the storm that caused her to enter. But soon she found herself inside. What ever it was, it was this action that would profoundly affect not only her future but also the fortunes of others.

As she pushed the door to the small store open it was accompanied by the sound of a small bell tinkling. Marilyn smiled to herself. Just like a Dickens novel, she thought. Nice touch.

"Can I help you or are your just trying to escape the weather," asked the forty something man with thick black hair tied into a cue at the nape of his neck?

Marilyn visibly jumped. Where had he come from? Then she noticed the doorway that led from a backroom behind him. His bright dark, almost black eyes seemed to be laughing in silent amusement.

"I'm sorry if I startled you," he said. "I have a habit of moving quietly. So much, that my friends have made me agree to clear my throat on a regular schedule so I don't sneak up on them unawares." He smiled, showing very regular, very straight teeth.

At first, Marilyn thought he might be laughing at her – but then she revised her opinion. Here was someone who enjoyed what he was doing and seemed to have discovered and be chuckling at the irony of life and be chuckling at its implications.

"I'm Samuel, you can call me Sam. I am the proprietor, janitor and chief stock boy of the famous bookstore you now stand in – 'The Druid's Grove.' And, as you can see," with this he pulled a business card out of thin air by legerdemain, "the founder of the Guild of Disreputable Sorcerers."

Marilyn looked down at the neatly calligraphed card he handed her. The Guild of Disreputable Sorcerers

"We're the one's you've been looking for!"

Marilyn smiled quietly to herself, sharing in Samuel's self-depreciating joke.

"Mind if I look around for a bit?"

"How could I deny a fair young lady seeking shelter from the storm? Especially, when she brings with her a ray of sunlight on such a dreary day."

Marilyn rolled her eyes as Sam simply shrugged his shoulders as if to say, "Yeah I know, I'm incorrigible and that line should be put out of its misery."

It was in the Druid's Grove that Marilyn came across a book entitled "A True and Faithful Relation of What Transpired for Many Years Between Doctor John Dee and Some Spirits", by Meric Causabon. This large tome, almost as big as a family bible, was hard to read, being written in the quaint style of the time of King

James. Nevertheless, she bought it because it told the fascinating and strange story of two Elizabethan magicians named John Dee and Edward Kelly. I described how the two occultists had devised a system for contacting supposedly angelic intelligences through the medium of a "shewstone". This crystal and associated materials are still on display in the British Museum in London. The angels dictated a great deal of information about a series of tablets written in an arcane language said to have been "spoken in heaven." Others theorized that it might be the language of sunken Atlantis.

Whatever its origin, it fired the imagination of Marilyn. She had previously read, in another book about how the ancient priestesses who were known as Pythonesses would communicate with their gods or goddesses via a dark crystal technique. She recalled St. Paul writing to the Corinthians about beholding God in " a glass darkly..."

Right then and there, she decided that she was going to pursue this path, alone or in a group. She hoped, of course, she could find members of her coven that would be as excited as she to explore this inner universe. But the direction this quest took was one that she could not have envisioned. She was to learn the dangers of pursuing the paths of power from instruction found in a book without the direction of a qualified and reliable teacher.

*   *   *   *   *

All of the members of the coven sat down on cushions scattered at regular intervals around the circle. In the center of this circle was a low altar supporting the usual symbols and weapons of the Craft. Marilyn approached the stand carrying a circular convex/concave, glossy, black mirror. She reached over on another table and produced a small crystalline pyramid of about twelve inches high. She placed it upon the altar and leaned the mirror against it so that it stood at an angle she could easily look into. She settled down upon her knees and prepared to make the invocation. She would be calling Hathor tonight, the ancient Egyptian Goddess of love and fertility.   All present were hopeful that a contact could be made through the mirror that would shed a blessing upon the entire group.

"Oh mighty Hathor! Come we beseech Thee! Ensoul our gathering with Thy healing and awakening influence…" Marilyn went on inspired by the idea that in ancient times seers would receive visions of the Shining Ones in a mirror very similar to the one she now gazed into that lay upon her altar.

All around her the fellow coven members had unconsciously began to breathe in rhythm with her cadence. As the call reached its climax, their adrenaline began to surge.

"Come unto me, great Goddess! I am Thy Priestess. Come unto me!"

The silence was total. The only sounds that could be heard around the circle were the popping of the incense and the expectant breathing of the participants. But it was not a passive silence. No, not at all. It was the type of silent listening you experience when you have awakened in the middle of the night because you think you have heard a sound downstairs and you thought you were alone in the house. It was expectant, searching, active.

They didn't know how long it had been manifesting before they noted it. Instead of an image forming in the mirror, a mist, almost a fog began to seep up from the floor of the chamber. Steadily it rose and began to swirl, whipping around each participant, seeking with an almost intelligent purpose.

Suddenly Marilyn collapsed and rolled partly over onto her side. From her mouth poured forth a string of words in a language that none present could know, except that the names Sekhmet, Apep and Anpu were repeated again and again. She screamed and leapt to her feet, standing ramrod straight, rigid. Simultaneously out of the mist, towering over the entire group sprang a giant Lion-headed figure.   This apparition thunderously roared -- suddenly all was black, the only sound the breaking of glass and the whimpering of someone in the darkness.

Marilyn's voice, sounding as if it were coming from far away, then broke through the darkness:

"I did not remove the Guardian! Khepher-Ra is still dwelling in the Duat? You must continue your journey to Amenti! Imhotep will guide him. He can be contacted at Saquara. I have been reborn in the lands past the setting sun. I dwell now beyond the City of the Golden Gates, beyond the sunken lands. My way is in the Waters!"

Someone found the light switch and turned it on. The scene revealed was that of chaos. The altar was turned over and the mirror lay broken upon the floor. The wine and cakes scattered around in fragments. The other members of the group were huddled singly or in couples against the walls. Only Marilyn was where she had been when the lights went out. She stood, staring down at the crystal pyramid she was holding in her hands. It was only when her brother Phillip shook her slightly that she seemed to revive and come to herself.

"What happened," she asked?

"Well, for one thing, you spoke in what I believe is ancient Egyptian. At least some of the words were from Khem," answered Phillip. "Other than that, nothing except a huge figure of the Goddess Sekhmet materialized and scared half the coven away. You'll have a hard time convincing anyone to attempt that particular experiment again! Are you all right? What do you remember?"

She paused, her brow wrinkling and then looked up confused: "All I can remember is someone accusing me of stealing something. They were threatening me with slavery if I did not return --- whatever it was. I don't remember. I wasn't afraid, but I know one thing for certain. The threat was not idle."

During the next eleven months, with ever-increasing severity Marilyn would lapse into these trances, speaking in an unknown language and not recovering for many minutes. It was always the same. She could only remember that someone - or something was threatening and accusing her of some theft or violation.

She discussed the situation with the nearest person she had to a teacher, Samuel. He would listen and advise her sometimes on some techniques she could try, everything from drinking a glass of blessed water to casting a circle with consecrated salt around her bed before going to sleep. Nothing seemed to dissuade the attacks.

Samuel, however, did help. He was the one to first make the observation that the attacks always occurred during the dark of the moon. Once the pattern was tied to the phases of the moon, Marilyn could fortify herself for her monthly battle.

Little by little, however, her vitality was being drained as evidenced by a slow loss of weight and energy till the faithful night when she could not be aroused. That was when Sam revealed to Phillip that he was a member of an organization that possessed among its membership individuals who had trained and dedicated their lives to the arcane sciences. These individuals had made the unreserved dedication and pledged to stand in the breach between innocents, like his sister and the forces of the Shadow that ever threatened to overwhelm them. Phillip pleaded with him to help and he agreed.

That night, after retiring to his apartment in the rear of his store and casting a consecrated circle, Samuel entered a trance. In this subconscious state, he sent his thoughts across space to another individual, also in trance. This individual's body lay upon a bier-like couch in his private temple a continent away just outside Los Angeles, California. His name was Arthur Alexander.

*   *   *   *   *

Arthur stopped into my on campus office, early in the morning. He smiled and offered me a large sized caramel ice coffee from the student union's coffee shop, together with a large Bavarian Crème.

"Okay, what's with the bribe," I asked smiling?

Feigning hurt, he answered. "I am just on my way to visit one of the most interesting and little known bookstores in Southern California. I, being the noble character I am, thought of my friend, Michael and stopped by to see if you would like to accompany me on my voyage of discovery. "

"Want company, huh? Where are we going," I asked, grabbing the proffered coffee and donut?

"Thanks Mike. The Jaguar is at the dealer for service and the other one is on loan to a friend who is showing it at a local auto show this week. As to where we're going. We need to head into Pasadena, to a bookstore across the street from the City College. You'll love it and, additionally, I'll spring for lunch at the restaurant of your choice, as long as it is somewhere along 'Restaurant Row' in Monrovia."

We drove along the 210 corridor under a perfect southern California sky, with the San Gabriel Mountains on our right and the cities of Arcadia and Rosemead on our left. Along the way he filled me in on the information he had received by his esoteric methods from Samuel, leaving out the details of the technique as he was pledged to do.

"Are you going to be able to help this poor girl?"

"I don't know. I'm going to have to do some research. There are a lot of the pieces of this particular puzzle that haven't been revealed to me. Hence, our current trip to a most unique bookstore.

"Then I'll probably have to invest in a plane ticket to the greater Boston area. And finally, it's quite in the cards that I may have to visit ancient Egypt."

"What do you mean 'Ancient' Egypt?"

"Perhaps I'll be able to tell you more about what I mean, if I have to seek the answers by that road," Arthur commented cryptically.

We pulled up to a small, independent bookshop directly across the street from the campus of City College. The sign touted "Books on Egyptology, Assyria and the Middle East." The Sign over the door proclaimed the establishment as "The Ancient Cultures Bookstore."

I peered into the dimly lit shop and all I could see was row after row of floor to ceiling bookcases, stuffed to capacity with volumes of every description – all used. I began to salivate. Here was an old fashion bookstore, one that was indeed rare to see these days, especially in Southern California. The big bookstore chains had made this type of niche store an endangered species. Most of the reading public were used to going into a well lighted, neatly categorized and arranged by marketing survey type of store. But here, here was a store that appealed to the soul who had a passion for the hunt, for the quest for those rare, out of print treasures that only the specialist would recognize.

Out of the back of the store a bushy bearded, older man emerged from the shadows. He may have been sixty-something, but there was not a strand of gray in his full leonine hair. Nor was their a tooth missing or discolored as evidenced by the flash of his winning grin as he approached.

"So, Traveler, you have decided to finally pay your poor brother a visit, huh," he said as he peered over the tops of his horn-rimmed glasses with the little shoestrings that ran from earpiece to earpiece and draped around his neck?

"My Frater," Arthur said, embracing the man with a big bear hug. "It has indeed been too long.

"May I introduce my friend Michael Richardson," he said gesturing to me. "Mike, this is the proprietor of this remarkable store, Saul Rubenstein. He has more Doctoral degrees than we'll ever see and could, and occasionally has, lectured to many so-called authorities at universities in the fields of Anthropology and Archeology. But more important he is my spiritual brother."

"Yeah, the 'black-sheep' of the family to be sure," Saul answered with a grin. "I'm very glad to meet you Michael."

Arthur explained to Saul the situation concerning Marilyn's condition as Sam had relayed to him on the inner planes the night before.

"Sounds as if she did not properly close the trance on the first occasion and has been gradually drawn into an existence on the Duat or lower astral," Saul offered as opinion.

"But there is something more than that, something we

cannot divine from the information available to us," said
Arthur.

"I'm sure the key to this mystery lies in the remote past,
perhaps in one of Marilyn's previous lives. That is why
I came to you. To see if anything in the narrative rang a
bell."

"Well, there was one thing that kind of attracted my
attention Arthur. Do you remember the comment
Marilyn made about her '
Place being in the waters?'"

Arthur nodded his understanding.

"Well, that is a line from the 'Chaldean Oracles' and is
many times thought to refer to the sinking of Atlantis."

"Yes and it was made in conjunction with a reference to
the 'City of the Golden Gates' and the sunken lands,"
said Arthur.

"But what does San Francisco have to do with ancient
Egypt," I asked?

They both looked at me in confusion and then
simultaneously burst out laughing.

"No, No my young friend," said Saul. The City of the
Golden Gates that I think it refers to, is the original city
on the, now vanished, island of Ruta in old Atlantis. It
was located on the sacred mountain and was defended

by large pylon gates plated in a highly bright colored metal, gold or, perhaps, oraculim. When the sun struck these gates they could be seen from miles around. Hence the appellation of the City of the Golden Gates in connection with the name of this ancient city.

"It has long been a theory that the civilization of Egypt originated with refugees fleeing the cataclysm of the sinking of this fabled continent."

Arthur continued: "You know Michael, that none of the main stream Egyptologists have been able to advance of satisfactory explanation for why the Old Kingdom suddenly seemed to spring onto the stage of civilization fully formed, with a complete system of Art, Culture, Literature, Writing, Medicine – you get the idea. All of these with no artifacts to show a developmental progression."

"Look at it this way," Saul said. " It's like finding the remains of a new Corvette automobile, and never seeing or finding, say a Ford T-model or any other earlier models that would show us a developmental evolution of the modern models."

"In fact," I answered, it is my understanding that Egyptian civilization declined from that period rather than evolved."

"That is correct," answered Saul. "There are some things we still cannot duplicate or equal that the Old Kingdom Dynasties did like the building of the Great

Pyramid, for example.

"But what further puzzles me," he continued, is the reference to a name that is normally associated with the Third dynasty. The name of Khepher-Ra."

Saul paused in silent thought. He then moved towards the section of the store that dealt with books on Egyptology. Scanning the shelves he took down a large, ribbed-spine volume entitled "Gaspar's Guide to Archeological Digs in the early half of the Twentieth Century."

"Let's see if Françoise can shed any light on that name. This book has an excellent index. Worth the price of the work by itself."

He flipped through the back pages, turning them back and forth until he found the reference he was looking for.

"Here it is. Just after the Second World War, Dr. Malcolm Bartholomew Makepeace, conducted a dig just outside the Saquara complex, where he discovered a previously unsuspected Third Dynasty tomb of a high priest of Khonsu, the Moon God. The Priest's name was Khepher-Ra. Odd name for a Moon priest, since it is made up of two names of Sun deities!"

"The Third Dynasty? That is the period of the Pharaoh Djoser or Zoser. Correct," I asked?

"Yes it is," answered Saul with an appraising glance. "But more importantly, it is the time of his high vizier, Imhotep, the great Egyptian sage."

"Imhotep, was later deified by the Egyptians," said Arthur. "According to the archives of the Inner Order, he was one of the Masters of the Third or Invisible Order. He undoubtedly is one of the greatest minds in all of Egypt's history."

"Here's something that may interest you," said Saul. "Several of the items from the tomb disappeared during transit to the Cairo Museum including the Mummy itself and a Lapis Lazuli Scarab that was embedded in a clear crystal pyramid. This was counted as a great loss because, according to the orthodox Egyptologists, the people of the Third or for that matter, any other dynasty had no technology to manufacture such a piece. It is still a mystery, and was theorized to be of a much earlier period than that of the tomb."

"At any rate there is another reference listed here in 'Explorations of the Third Dynasty' by Makepeace himself. "

Saul returned the large volume to the shelf and ran his thumb on a higher shelf. Finally he brought over a step stool and pulled another, smaller book from its place.

Ah, here it is," he said triumphantly. "This will give us a little more detailed information about the dig.

Something is tickling the back of my brain on this. Something interesting, but I can't quite get it to focus." He fell into silence as he scanned the pages in the smaller book until he found the reference he was searching for.

I thought so. There was a scandal of sorts connected with that dig. Sort of tarnished the reputation of Makepeace, although he was never directly implicated."

"What happened," I asked?

One of Makepeace's assistance, A Said Al-Makesh, was later implicated in theft and smuggling of ancient artifacts. Let me see," with this he pulled down another book and quickly found the reference he was seeking.

"Just as I remembered. The Al-Makesh family made quite a stir about five years later when it was discovered that they had built their country house right over the entrance to an unsuspected tomb. They had been looting that ruin of all of its artifacts and selling them on the black market."

"Very clever. They could work on the site at night and nobody would suspect a thing because they were essentially invisible. The site being hidden by their basement!"

"How long before they got caught," Arthur asked?

"They didn't. The authorities found the evidence after

they had disserted the house and immigrated to Switzerland! They got completely away!”

“You suspect that the missing items from the Khepher-Ra tomb found it’s way into the black market via the Al-Makesh family operation,” I asked?

“Perhaps,” answered Arthur. “It would explain the presence of the crystal pyramid and scarab. But how did the jewel come into the possession of a young women in Massachusetts.”

“One other thing,” Saul said, looking up from Makepiece’s book. “The ‘Jewel’ according to the Professor is supposed to be cursed. It is supposed to be haunted by the Goddess Sekhmet which is usually represented as having the head of a lion.”

* * * * *

“This, indeed looks like to the Jewel of Khepher-Ra,” Arthur said as he looked at the scarab laden crystal pyramid I was holding in my hands.

 We had flown into Logan International airport earlier that day and had driven to Samuel’s shop and thence to Marilyn’s family home near Cape Ann. Phillip had been expecting us and had ushered us into the library where we were introduced to Marilyn’s parents.

“I’m puzzled as how this artifact came into the

170

possession of Marilyn," I asked?

"It was a gift, an inheritance from our great uncle Malcolm," answered Phillip.

"Malcolm as in Malcolm Makepeace, Dr. Malcolm Makepeace," I asked?

"Yes," answered Marilyn's father. "Malcolm is my wife's uncle. Her maiden name is Makepeace. Why?"

I let out a long low whistle. Arthur filled the rest of the group in on the information we had discovered at Saul's, including the bit of information about the crystal being haunted.

"Some inheritance," said Phillip.

"Chances are your great uncle didn't believe the story. After all, he didn't have any problem with the artifact, did he?" Arthur looked around at the heads shaking no.

"It wasn't until Marilyn's group used the Jewel in conjunction with the invocation that the trouble started. Evidently it somehow activated the properties of the artifact," said Samuel.

"I knew that these ridiculous beliefs and practices would lead to trouble," Marilyn's father said.

"Mr. Dixon," Arthur said, "What would happen if someone crossed two wires when rewiring a lamp plug and then turned on the power?”

“They might get a shock. Might cause a fire. Why?”

“And what would be the cause of that shock?”

“Probably, ignorance of the proper way to wire the plug.”

“Exactly. It wouldn’t be the current’s fault and we wouldn’t go back to candles because of it, would we?”

“Okay. I surrender. What you’re saying is that it is our ignorance of these laws that is causing the problem and that; once we understand them we might derive benefit from their application. Is that it?”

“Mr. Dixon, the reason your children feel comfortable with considering alternate ways of looking at life is because you and your wife have instilled in them a sense of adventure and a confidence in their abilities to handle the unknown. All Marilyn needs right now is some education. That’s why my friends and I are here. We will help you get to the bottom of all this.”

“Anything I or my family can do to assist you, just let us know,” Marilyn’s father said.

“As a matter of fact, if I could borrow the Jewel of Khepher-Ra, it will speed up things considerably. I can’t guarantee that I will be able to return it to you though,” Arthur responded.

"If it will help, you can keep the damn thing. It apparently has brought us nothing but grief."

"Tonight," said Arthur turning to his Fraters, "we pay a visit to the Hall of the Archives."

* * * * *

Thus, later that night Arthur, Samuel and I were gathered in Samuel's apartment behind the Druid's Grove. Arthur had skipped dinner, electing to fast so that he would be more receptive for the work he was going to undertake.

It was well after midnight before he judged it sufficiently quiet to cast his circle of protection and enter into the trance that would take him to the "Court of the Seekers" and the Fraternity's Astral Temple.

I sat beside Arthur's temporarily vacated body with a tape recorder running, recording all that he described of the vision. But, perhaps because of my close work with him over the past couple of years I felt myself also slipping into his trance. And, through this rapport I began to see the experience through his eyes.

We entered the temple precincts much as I had experienced before with Arthur. As we passed the "Avenue of the Sphinxes" we turned to he right and made our way over the slight rise to the "Hall of the Archives". But instead of the familiar Keeper of the

Records, Frater "S" being there to welcome us we were confronted by a reddish-brown skinned individual dressed in the robes of a High Priest of Heliopolis. A sense of great power radiated from this person just as you can sense power radiating from a high voltage electrical transformer. You could feel the hum in the air. He smiled at us as we approached him and introduced himself, simply:

 "I am Imhotep."

I stopped, totally still for at least ten seconds. Imhotep was looking directly at me. Arthur seemed to note for the first time that I had been drawn into the inner planes with him

"My brothers," the ancient Egyptian sage said, "I've elected to meet you here because of the importance of the issue at hand. I also have a distinctly personal, karmic interest in this affair."

"Master Imhotep," Arthur answered, "we are honored by your reception and will assist you in anyway we can. But how does a cursed artifact, stolen from a tomb affect your karma?"

"The instrument you know as the Jewel of Khepher-Ra is much more important than you could be expected to know.

"This artifact resided, at one time, in my tomb at Saqqara. However, it is much, much older than that

174

complex. In fact, part of the holy precincts of that complex was constructed with the agreement of the pharaoh Djoser, at my urging to house that Jewel.

"To understand the importance of the pyramid shaped stone you must come with me into the Hall of the Mists."

Arthur looked at me and nodded. We then followed the white-robed priest through the portal into that part of the Hall of the Archives where events in the Akashic Records, the memory of all past events could be viewed.

It is called the "Hall of the Mists" because, for most people, it had the appearance of a room of swirling, veiled, impenetrable fog. For those with knowledge of the technique, I had been informed, the fog would clear and they could view events of times long past and garner the necessary information to complete tasks allotted to them.

As we followed Imhotep into the mist-filled corridor, I experienced a swooping sensation of vertigo and would have become totally disoriented if it had not been for the firm grasp of Arthur's hand upon my shoulder. The feeling of being in many places at once passed quickly and the silvery-gray curtain parted to reveal an exotic scene of ancient times, times now lost to the shadowy stories of legends.

Revealed was a large, flat plateau with a long, broad procession way that ran from an immense pyramid straight as an arrow to a gigantic golden plated pylon gate that soared over one hundred feet above the surface. Row upon row of white-robed priests and priestesses were lined up in silent, alert expectation, awaiting some event. The hour as attested by the rose glow increasing upon the sea-swept horizon in the distance was just before dawn.

As the disk of the sun broke out of the sea, the voices of the assembled initiates joyfully trumpeted forth in the measured cadences of a hymn:

> "O Atum the creator of Ra,
> You become high in the heavens!
> You rise up as the Benben Stone in
> Mansion of the Phoenix in Heliopolis!"

"The Heliopolis that they speak of was not of Khem," said Imhotep. "It was an older, more ancient city that gave birth to my home. It was the one that sent forth seedbearers carrying to keys to the Great Tradition before the sea claimed them and drowned the ancient temple of the sun.

"Look," he pointed behind us

We turned and saw the first rays of the sun reflected and amplified by a crystal pyramidion set upon a golden capstone. This crystal formed the apex of the large, pyramid-shaped temple. The crystal seemed to shimmer with an aura of its own that was independent of the beams of sunlight that struck it.

"It was here, in Heliopolis on the island of Ruta in the fabled continent of lost Atlantis that all three primary rays met. That Jewel on the tip of the great Sun Temple focused these great aspects of consciousness and Nature for the benefit of humanity.

"That crystal was one of the items entrusted to the high priest Helios by the Manu Narada just before they opened the Elemental Gates that sent the Island to beneath the ocean. He carefully transported it to the plains of Giza in ancient Khem."

"What happened to it then, Master," asked Arthur?

"It was judged that the conditions were not right for the three great rays to be again united. So it was enshrined in a temple in the new Heliopolis, a temple known as the 'Mansion of the Phoenix.'"

"Then the Jewel of Khepher-Ra is ..." Arthur started.

"Yes," finished Imhotep. "It is the Benben stone."

*   *   *   *   *

After we returned to our bodies, over a cup of steaming, hot coco, Arthur filled Samuel in on the details of the vision.

"But how did the Jewel end up in the tomb of Khepher-

Ra," asked Samuel?

"When it became evident to Imhotep and the other senior adepts of the third dynasty that the Benben's great power might fall into the hands of those likely to abuse it, they decided on a strategy to insure it would be safe," replied Arthur.

"They removed it from the Mansion of the Phoenix and secretly placed it in a tomb of an unknown priest."

"That of Khepher-Ra," interrupted Samuel.

"Yes, this tomb was in the Saqqara complex, but its exact location was a closely kept secret. No funeral ceremony was performed, because Khepher-Ra was, in reality, Imhotep! And the reason the mummy was lost and presumed stolen is the fact that there was never any mummy to begin with!"

'I don't understand," said Samuel.

"Because, my brother. Khepher-Ra is Imhotep and he is one of the Adepts who have completed the Great Work. Imhotep has never died. He has been in continuous incarnation, more or less, since the time of the pharaoh Djoser. That is also why his tomb has never been found by Egyptologists."

"That's incredible," Samuel exclaimed! "Why did he invent someone like Khepher-Ra?"

"That was a deception that the whiley, old Djoser came up with to act as a cover story. They didn't want the secret resting place of the Benben stone to leak out. So they placed it in the tomb of a fictional priest in the middle of the night. Only the highest of the Priesthood knew its location and the means of entry. The secret was passed down from high priest to high priest of Heliopolis until the Theban priesthood supplanted them as the 'official state religion'. The location was completely lost at the end of the 18th dynasty when Aknanton was over thrown. That famous pharaoh caused a great stir in the political structure of Khem by pledging his allegiance to Heliopolitan system and making public the worship of the one God. The politically entrenched Theban priesthood, of course, could not tolerate the major loss of power and prestige and arranged for an insurrection.

"When Makepeace unearthed the Benben stone just after the Second World War, he had no idea of what he had found. The sarcophagus was opened and inside instead of a third dynasty mummy, he found an archeological anomaly - A crystal pyramid with an embedded scarab, an artifact that could not have been produced by the people of that period.

"He did not want to risk his professional reputation by producing the artifact and thus calling into question the accepted chronology of the civilization of Egypt so he fabricated the theft story. The Al-Malak family, although guilty of much smuggling and theft, had nothing to do with the disappearance of the Jewel.

"Even though it is traumatic that Marilyn received such a shock when she accidentally activated the stone's power, it is, in a way, fortunate."

"How can this be fortunate," Sam asked?

"Because," Arthur continued," the time and stars are right for the Benben stone to resume its function of uniting the three rays. The Sun now rises in the sign of the Water Bearer.

"Marilyn acted as sort of a locator beacon of the artifact. You see, the Heliopolitan priesthood, which still has members today, had lost track of the Jewel! She has given them information at a critical time, information necessary for them to fulfill their mission."

"But how is this all going to affect Marilyn? Is she doomed to exist in this half –life, coma-like state of trance?"

"That depends, to a large extent on her. She must make a decision. Imhotep stated that she would have to visit the Hall of Dual Truth on the inner planes. She will have to face the Judgment of Maat, which he had no doubt she would emerge victorious.

"However, she will then be asked to perform an additional task. She will be asked to redeem her freedom by undertaking to return the stone to a hidden chapel near Saqqara. If she accepts, she will awaken and will play a major part in the spiritual awakening of this New Age. If she accepts, it will be our task as initiates of the same tradition of the Mysteries of Heliopolis to smooth her way and assist her in any way we can."

*   *   *   *   *

When they had returned to Cape Ann, they found Marilyn had regained consciousness and was setting up, enjoying a lunch of soup and sandwiches.

"Well, you seemed to have recovered," said Samuel. "I'd like to introduce…"

"Greetings, Frater who dwells within the Mystic Mountain." Marilyn's interruption by giving the formal greeting of an initiate to the visible head of the order stunned everyone present into silence.

They looked at her closely and it was apparent that her ordeal on the inner planes had altered her. No longer was she the immature, college graduate who experimented with the esoteric sciences. No, a subtle transformation had occurred. There was a firming of the lines around her eyes and mouth. When she looked at you the impression of unaffected confidence shown forth. Before, where she would have been described as pretty, now all would agree she possessed true beauty. An inner power radiated from within. She spoke and

181

moved with poise.

"The Priestess of Khem has awakened," observed Arthur.

"Yes," replied Marilyn. "Many of the memories, like parts of a jig-saw puzzle are coming together.

"We must return the stone to its throne in the Mansion of the Phoenix," she continued. "The Great Ones told me that you would be willing to assist. They also told me that this must be accomplished before the new moon of the Vernal Equinox."

"How are we going to get that chunk of crystal past Customs in Egypt," I asked, shaking my head?

"Daoud, our Cairo temple chief will assist us," Arthur answered. "Besides, Customs inspectors will be looking for artifacts leaving the country more than the other way around."

"The priests of Heliopolis will also smooth the way," said Marilyn, with a cryptic smile. "But the primary responsibility will still be ours.

"I was told, " she continued, "That the customs officials would be the least of our worries. There are other dangers. Now that the Jewel has been activated, we must have it properly restored upon its throne. It would not do for it to activate upon a crowded airliner. We should have time if we act promptly.

"Even so, there are other dangers. Your assistance will involve great risk. Are you prepared to take such a challenge?"

Arthur responded first: "I have made the Unreserved Dedication; but you, my friends," he turned to Samuel and me, "You should not feel compelled to enter a quest that could put your lives or sanity in jeopardy. The Way of the Phoenix will be well guarded."

"I am an initiate," said Samuel. "I have vowed to serve the Light."

They turned to me. I answered: "Although I am not an initiate in this lifetime I wouldn't miss this adventure for a million dollars! Count me in."

*　*　*　*　*

The "adventure" went well as far as the transport of the crystal artifact back to Egypt. It was decided to register it as a new age art object and, as such we breezed through customs. As agreed, Daoud, the Fraternity's chief in Cairo met us at the airport; but as for the legendary priesthood of ancient Heliopolis, it seemed that they were remaining a legend. At least they'd not made their entrance upon the stage of this play as of yet.

Daoud had engaged two brothers Said and Ahmed to act

as guides and provide the transportation from our hotel that was located near Giza to the Saqqara complex just to the southwest of the ruins of Memphis. My vision of crossing the desert on the backs of camels was thankfully transformed into a short trip in two Grand Cherokees moving along paved highways. However, as we passed the ancient avenue of the sphinxes and could see in the distance, illuminated by the silvery light of the waning moon and the millions of stars, we caught site of the stepped pyramid of Djoser. It was easy to imagine the great empire that reined during the period of the Old Kingdom thousands of years past. The wind was lightly blowing, sending the sands whispering around us. In my imagination, I could hear the plaintive call of the jackals standing sentinel in the surrounding vastness.

We dismounted and stood looking at the shadowy stone mountains looming in the darkness. Marilyn turned round a full circle, gazing in the direction of the mastabas in frustration.

"Things have changed much in the five thousand years since my memories. I'm not sure…I'm sorry, but I'm just not sure."

"Perhaps we may assist the Priestess," said Ahmed, unexpectantly?"

Everyone turned and stared open mouthed at the two brothers.

Bowing, Ahmed continued: "We are the 'Manunfu Benu', the 'Guardians of the Phoenix' and successors of the Priests of Inunu."

You are the current day Priests of Heliopolis," I asked in disbelief?

"Yes, we guard the way of the Phoenix," Said answered. "All of us have been waiting a long time for the Jewel of Khepher-Ra to be returned to our safe keeping."

"All of you," asked Samuel?

"To be sure." Ahmed made a wide gesture and ten other men, all robed in white stepped from the shadows into the light. "We will also guard you as you restore the sacred stone to the throne of the Benben.

"Come, the entrance to the hidden chapel is near the 'House of the North', past the great Processional Way."

We followed Ahmed, his flashlight illuminating our way along the Processional Way and across the East Court. The bobbing lights of the lamps cast weird shadows as they reflected upon the statues located there.

Just as we entered one of the porticos, immediately inside the threshold, Said halted and reached into one of the many cracks in the sandstone masonry. With a visible effort, he pushed hard. A click sound followed by the echoing of stone scraping against stone could be heard. A pavement flag, just off the walkway yawned open, revealing a series of steps descending into an abyss of darkness.

"Thou risest, thou risest, and thou comst forth from the god Nun…O Thou divine child, who didst create thyself, I am not able to describe thee," Marilyn proclaimed to everyone's surprise.

It was apparent that Marilyn had slipped into a semi-hypnotic trance. The personality of the ancient priestess had assumed temporary dominance, once again.

The two brothers bowed to her and began unpacking the crate in which the Benben resided. Then, with Marilyn preceding them, they began carrying the stone down the stairs.

I moved to light their way with my flashlight, but to my amazement, the corridor began to brighten before them.

"The ever-burning lamps of Heliopolis," said Arthur. "I'd heard of them but never thought I would see one."

"We retain much of the ancient wisdom of Khem," said Said. "But alas, we have lost much more. Still, we remain as guardians of that wisdom until the time comes when humanity is ready, once again, to use the knowledge wisely."

We moved down a wider corridor flanked by pairs of statues of the gods of the great "Ennead of Heliopolis."

Marilyn, in a state of ecstasy recited one of the "utterances" of the ancient liturgy known as the "Pyramid Texts":

"Atum-Khepher, you have climbed to the summit of the mountain. You have mounted the Benben stone in the Mansion of the Phoenix in Iunu. You manifested Shu, you created Tefnut, and you put your arms around them, you embraced them so that your ka might ensoul them. O thou great nine, which is in Iunu, by your names – Atum, Shu, Tefnut, Geb, Nut, Osiris, Isis, Set, Nephthys – children of Atum, extend his heart to these, your children. In your name of Nine Bows."

As she finished the invocation, she made a gesture of blessing towards the end of the corridor and, seemingly, in response the wall slid, soundlessly down into a slot in the floor revealing a brightly illuminated chapel.

At the center of this chapel, framed by the doorway stood a large, truncated pyramid, some seven feet on a side, tapering to a platform that would perfectly accommodate the crystal pyramidion, the Benben stone that Said and Ahmed carried.

This pyramid that awaited the Jewel was completely covered with gold plate and bore on each side in low relief the arms of the Ka with the ancient Eye of Ra.

Said and Ahmed slowly set their burden into its palace upon the golden pyramid, the throne of the Phoenix.

Immediately the crystal began to vibrate as three colored rays radiated from it accompanied by three corresponding, mystical notes. The first was golden with a hundred voices that seemed to sing "Ahhhhh". Closely following a red ray shot forth with a chorus of "oooooo". Finally, a blue radiance became visible accompanied by a vibrating "mmmmmm". The three colors swirled to ultimately combine in an aura of pure, white light. The chamber was infused with a mystical, energy that seemed to awaken our consciousness, lift the veil from our eyes and lift us to another, higher order of perception.

However, just as the trio of colors and sound started to combine the lights within the chamber were extinguished leaving the room only dimly illuminated by the lamps in the outer passageway.

Suddenly, it was before the three in the chamber. A large, lion-headed creature towering over us, thundering forth a roar that echoed again and again in the subterranean chapel.

The two brothers quickly stumbled back, throwing their arms across their faces as if to ward off this ferocious guardian.

The entity discarded its lion-headed mask and revealed itself as a large fire elemental.

"Aaii," screamed Ahmed, "a Djinn!" He and Said turned to flee. Samuel moved to interpose himself between Marilyn and the angry elemental just as it shot forth its rage in a bright curtain of flame directed upon him and the two priests.

Marilyn raised her hands in invocation; Arthur and Daoud raised theirs in a strange gesture that later I was told was the sign of an initiate of the element of fire.

"O Great Isis! I call to Thee for Thy protection," Marilyn's voice rose above the confusion. "I am Thy priestess! Answer unto me!"

Suddenly between the fire elemental and her shown the form of a glowing ankh – the emblem of the key of life. The guardian djinn released and banished by this seal of Isis, disintegrated into a thousand sparks whirling away into the Unmanifest.

The Benben began to glow once again, but softly this time as compared to before. We rushed forweard to he two brothers but their chared remains left little doubt as to their fate.

We turned toward Marilyn who was holding the body of Samuel in her arms; rocking him as you might a baby. His blistered face and sightless eyes staring blindly at us.

"What happened to the light? It's so dark in here. Did we get the Benben back upon its throne? I can hear the beautiful music; but I can't see that radiance.

*   *   *   *   *

Sam's optic nerves had been burned, the examining Doctor in Cairo later said, much like someone who had looked unprotected at an arc welder. Marilyn swore she would become his eyes. The awakening of her memories had also made her aware of a link between them that had endured over many, many lives.

The Guardians of the Phoenix mourned the passing of Ahmed and Said. We all attended their requiem. During the "Ritual of Birth," Marilyn in their honor spoke the words of blessing – ancient words that had came down from the lost continent. I'll translate them into English:

> "Carry their souls down the sacred river.
> May its holy currents bring them to Life,
> Light and Love. So mote it be!

A QUESTION OF HONOR

Sometimes appearances can be extremely deceptive. A calm neighborhood can veil ancient and powerful mysteries. In a section of Los Angeles bordered on the south by Franklin Avenue near the famous "Magic Castle" and on the east by the perhaps even more famous "Hollywood Bowl" lies a quiet tangle of winding, hillside cul-de-sacs known as the Mount Olympus district. Here, white-stucco, neo-classical villas compete with California, ranch style houses to accentuate the beautiful, tree shrouded lanes that promise to lead over the hill – but never quite deliver on the promise. Still, even if you don't make it all the way to Muholland Drive, the picturesque journey with signs proclaiming: "Please go slow. We have baby Deer!" is a reward unto itself. It is hard to believe that just a few blocks below, the rush and struggle of old Hollywood is always underway.

But here, on this hill is an enigma. In the midst of this maze of streets, toward the hilltop, rests a greystone,

Tudor mansion. It sits behind its tall stonewalls and wrought iron gates on a modest ten acres of garden grounds.

The young people in the neighborhood don't climb these walls, even though one would think that the gardens offered a perfect place to act out "dungeons and dragons" adventures. It isn't that they are afraid of the place, but for some reason, it just doesn't occur to them to trespass.

Once, however, some young lads attempted to pursue a mis-thrown Frisbee that had, in the early evening, found its way over the wall into the lawn beyond. They had been intimidated they explained later by a strange looking, large, black dog with the longest ears. When they rang at the front gate, the smiling, friendly gardener escorted them to their wayward disk. He informed the boys that the property kept no such watchdog.

The boy's wonder was only increased when they later compared their dog with a picture in a book in their school library showing a depiction of the Jackal-headed god Annubis. They agreed it looked very similar to the type of dog they saw in the gathering gloom. But the neighbors wouldn't keep a Jackal – would they?

The ownership of the surrounding homes might change from time to time with their realtor signs making an appearance and then vanishing just as fast. But no one could recall this particular property going on the market. In fact, if the records were consulted at the County Hall of Administration, it would have revealed that this house and grounds had predated most, if not the entire surrounding neighborhood, the others building up around it. And, in over one hundred years, it had never changed hands. It had always housed and had been owned by an organization known simply as the "Abiegnus Foundation".

The purpose of the foundation seems to lie somewhere in the areas of research, educational and charitable. No one outside of this organization seems to know exactly what type of research, etc. it was engaged in. Even the United States government didn't seem to have much of an interest.

At various times of the month, a modest group of men and women would gather, usually in the evening for study. But the individuals could never be drawn into conversation about the aims of the Foundation, other than to point out its generous donations to the many local charities, hospitals and organizations for the support of the arts.

No, these people wouldn't say much. Because they were all members of "The Fraternity", an ancient, worldwide society dedicated to serving the forces of the Light and aiding the evolution of the consciousness of humanity. Presently Dr. Arthur Alexander as "Steward" physically headed this Fraternity. But, as his title suggests, he was merely the servant of those of far greater attainment.

I had been an initiate of The Fraternity for approximately one year when the strange case of Geoffrey Wall occurred. Geoffrey was a young man in his twenties with his whole life before him. But he was destined to be tested early. I first met him while we were both doing research in the library at the mansion. He introduced himself with a shy, self-drepreciatory smile:

"Pardon me, Dr. Richardson, isn't it?"

"Please call me Mike," I answered. "After all, we are members of the same spiritual family or we wouldn't be here you know, 'Who is my mother if not the Lodge? And who are my brothers and sisters but the initiates thereof?'"

"Thank you doctor – ah Mike. Frater Jacob, the Archivist, mentioned that you might assist me. I'm looking for a book that you seemed to have checked out. It is the only copy."

"I wouldn't be surprised," I answered, looking at the foot high stack of volumes piled in front of me on the table. "Which one do you need?"

"Ah, Causabon's 'True and Faithful Relation'." He gestured to a very large, three-inch thick volume bound in leather.

"Oh, you're researching Dee. Me too. But, I'm finished with that source, so no problem."

"That's very nice of you. If it would be okay, I'll just sit across from you. That way, if you need it, it will still be right here."

Saturday morning passed slowly as we consulted book after book in our related areas of research. Finally, a loud "grumbling" of my new acquaintance's stomach announced that lunchtime had arrived. We decided that perhaps it would be nice to grab a bite at the "Pig-n-whistle" down the hill on Hollywood Boulevard.

As we ate our lunch I noticed that Geoff seemed to be preoccupied. Finally, after much apparent inner debate, he appeared to come to a decision and launched into conversation with a question:

"Mike, since you became an initiate, has your life seemed more turbulent, more full of tests?"

"Well, it certainly has been more interesting. Why?"

"I guess I thought that entering the Fraternity would place the Keys of the Kingdom in my hands. Instead, I've been given a whole new set of locks!"

"Yeah, it sometimes sure seems like that. I remember, Arthur Alexander once explained to me that often times because of the increase in energy after initiation the first thing that appears to happen to a neophyte is that he gets himself into trouble."

"Well, that's certainly true in my case," he answered.

Geoff seemed to withdraw into himself after this rather mysterious comment.

I didn't see or hear again from my young frater until several months later when Arthur Alexander handed me a wedding invitation. It looks like Geoff had found the keys to some of his new locks, at least in the area of relationships, for the announcement was an invitation to attend the wedding of Geoff and his soon to be bride, Jessica.

"This is surprising," I said to Arthur. "I barely know Frater Wall. I only met him on one occasion."

"Yes, but you or rather what you told him over lunch made a deep impression on him."

"Lunch? You know about our conversation?"

"I've become very familiar with the tests young Geoff has been going through. I believe your comments gave him the idea to approach me.

"Let me tell you his story."

* * * * *

Geoffrey came into the Fraternity after studying the esoteric sciences for many of his teenage years. He was one of those souls who hear the call of "deep calling to deep" almost from the cradle, so to speak. He and his boyhood friend, Oscar had shared many adventures scouring used bookstores in search of rare, arcane texts. They would share the costs of these books, often times sacrificing their lunch money or paying for the books by the lay away plan.

Oscar and Geoff became best friends until Oscar left for the Marines. When he returned after his "hitch" was up, he had changed. He was distant, hardened, calculating with a cynicism that looked out upon the world with a soured view.

Geoff recounted to me a conversation they had that illustrated this. Oscar had noticed a book Geoff had left open on his desk. It was "The True and Invisible Rosicrucian Order" by Paul Foster Case.

"Why are you wasting your time with this junk," asked Oscar?

"Junk! I've found it to be one of the best books I've come across on initiation and the grade system," answered Geoff.

"That's your problem. You've never got out on your own. You feel that you need the cuddling of a group or order to hold your hand. You don't need a lodge. You can make just as much progress by yourself. All it takes is a strong will and determination---and the right books." With these last words he threw down a copy of "The Satanic Bible" on top of Case's book.

"There's a book that comes closer to the reality of the world. It isn't how we thought it was when we were teenagers, Geoff. It's a survival test! If you don't seize your opportunities and get your share, somebody else will get it and you'll be left looking stupid as the train pulls out."

"What's that supposed to mean," Geoff asked?

"It means, my naïve young seeker, that the high minded attitudes we espoused as immature teenagers were bullshit! What's the use of having this inside, hidden knowledge if your not going to use it to your advantage? Like the book says, somewhere," he picked up the satanic book, "if someone gets in your way— smash him!

"And that goes for anyone. In the war of life, your either for me or 'agin' me, as they say."

As time passed, Oscar became more cynical –and ruthless. The two friends began quarreling when he found he couldn't he couldn't convert Geoff to his schemes. Oscar started running with a rougher crowd and, despite his brags about not needing anyone he ended up joining one of the darker local groups.

When Geoff entered our Fraternity and had the poor discrimination to tell his friend about it, it was almost more then Oscar could stand.

"It is beyond me," Oscar ranted, "why you still feel you need this archaic, self righteous group of old ladies. What have they taught you? Won't tell, huh. That's because you don't have anything worth telling about. It isn't until you get into their precious Greater Mysteries that you'll ever learn anything of value – anything really powerful"

"You don't know anything about them," answered Geoff. "Your only guessing from what you read about them in books."

"Oh, is that so?" I'll let you in on a little secret. Last month, my group did a little Magick, much more than you will have attempted. We performed an evocation from the "Lesser Key of Solomon." We used a drugged-out street prostitute as our medium. Put her right in the Triangle of Art. The demon, speaking through her told us about a Greater Mystery document."

"You did what? You placed another human being in the Triangle so she would become possessed by an entity of the Qlippoth!"

"She hardly counts as a fellow human, Geoff. She was a street whore, a junkie. Besides, we paid her for the use of her body."

"I can't believe you. I think we better just agree to part ways."

"Maybe, but not until you help me get a hold of that document the demon told me about.""

"And why would you in your wildest dreams ever think I would violated my initiation oath and help you do that?"

"Because if you don't, the next 'volunteer' to serve in the triangle might just be your lady love, Jessica. Don't shake your head, my friend. At the very least, my friends and I could make her and your life a living hell. And forget about going to the cops. The story you would have to tell them would just get you certified and then Jessica would be all mine. I kind of fancy her anyway."

Geoff tried to land a right cross onto his former friend's jaw, but Oscar's combat training exceeded Geoff's skill and he easily blocked it and put Geoff on his back.

Looking down on him with a self-satisfied smirk, Oscar told him:

"Don't get so upset. None of this needs to happen. All you have to do is smuggle out the document to me tomorrow night. Just sneak into the ritual vault that must exist in the library, at least according to the demon, and remove a document known as the 'Ritual of the Three Ways." I'll be waiting at this address," Oscar passed him a slip of paper. " If you do as you have been told, then we'll part in peace. Screw-up and I promise you Jessica's hell will just begin in that triangle. Understand? Oh, and by the way. One word of this to anyone, including your Fraters or Sorors, and it will be the last you see of sweet Jessica. Count on it."

With Geoff's shaky assent, Oscar nodded and left.

Geoff didn't know what to do. Reluctantly, he made his way to the mansion and tried to calm himself by reading in the library He watched Frater Jacob, go about his tasks while pretending to study some of the First Order documents. He noted that the Archivist would leave the room with the Ritual vault unattended for long periods of time. Why should he worry about the security of the documents? Everyone in the large building was a handpicked individual. Additionally, all had been initiated and taken a solemn oath of integrity. The thought of violating that obligation literally made Geoff ill. Still, Oscar's threats kept echoing in his ear. He had no doubt, after hearing the account of the prostitute, that Oscar and his friends would seriously hurt Jessie.

Geoffrey felt that he had no option, no alternative. Jacob had gone upstairs to one of the Guardian's office. He drifted over to the Ritual room and ducked in while no one else was in the room. He had never been in this room before and it took him a while to figure out which system that the rituals, knowledge and explanatory lectures were arranged. Finally he spotted a bound document, very old from the look of it. It was embossed with the symbol of the Second Order and bore the title, "The Ritual of the Three Ways", just as Oscar's demon had described. He didn't pick it up. He didn't want to take a chance of someone discovering it to be missing. He would wait till just before closing tomorrow. He hurried out into the general reading room, just barely avoiding being caught by Rabbi Bergman.

Breathing rapidly, with perspiration beading on his brow, Geoff hurriedly packed up his briefcase and left the mansion. Tomorrow, he would have to violate his honor to save the one he loved.

* * * * *

The evening gloom found Geoffrey huddled at his usual spot in the great library of the mansion. Despite his best efforts to alter the flow of time, the clock still ticked off its interminable minutes, one at a time. He glanced alternatively at the deepening night reflecting into the large French windows that opened out onto the garden and the old Jewish man seated at the Archivist's desk in the book lined room with increasing apprehension for the distasteful task that he had set before himself.

Finally Frater Jacob got up and walked over to him.

"I'm going to get a bite to eat," he said, giving Geoff an affectionate pat on the shoulder. "Would you like to join me or could I bring you back a snack?"

"Uh no, thank you Jacob. I'll be finished in just a minute or two. Then I'm supposed to meet a friend down the hill. Thanks anyway."

He felt horrible, lying to the kindly old man, who had almost adopted him as a son of the spirit. But, as far as it went, he had told him the truth.

202

Jacob nodded and walked out of the door down the hall toward the Dining Hall. Now was his chance. Evidently everybody else also was at dinner. He sprang up and moved rapidly to the door of the restricted room. To his astonishment, when he looked on the shelf where he had found the ritual yesterday evening he found a vacant space. Suppressing the urge to panic, he frantically looked around. It was then that he noticed the bound copy with its tell tale marking lying on the bottom of a stack of rituals and lectures on the librarian's desk. He retraced his steps and with some difficulty extracted the book from the documents piled on top of it.

Hurrying before someone came in and discovered him with the book in his hands, he moved toward the door and started to turn in the direction of the door. To his horror, he observed Rabbi Bergman and Dr. Alexander walking deep in conversation towards him. Hesitating only for a moment, Geoff reversed direction and walked rapidly the other way toward the Hall of the Lesser Mysteries. He could, he reasoned cross through it and out its back door and make his way around to the front by the shrubbery.

He passed through the antechamber with all of the photographs of the past guardians and entered the Hall of Initiation. He was just moving around the altar, using the red votive light as his beacon when a voice called out of the gloom to him. He froze.

A cold tingle started at the small of his back and slowly worked its way up his spine onto the hairs on the back of his neck. He turned in the direction of the voice and saw a white-robed shadow emerge slowly into the light. He must have been in his early seventies but his step betrayed no hint of feebleness or infirmity. Rather the ease of his movements spoke of a vitality of a man decades younger. He was of medium height, stockily built with small expressive hands. As he moved further into the light, Geoff noticed he was wearing a gold pentagram lamen suspended from a golden chain about his neck. But the most distinctive features were his hair, beard and eyes. His bald dome glistened in the uneven light of the overhead spirit lamp. His head was fringed by a ring of shoulder-length, snow-white hair and complemented by a matching, full-length beard. His clear, blue eyes seem to twinkle in amusement as he spoke:

"I'm sorry youngin. I wasn't trying to ambush you. But I have been waiting for you."

"For me. What for?"

"Well, first off, it concerns the book you hold in your hands. No, no need to try to conceal it. I'm not going to have you arrested or expelled or any such thing.

"Additionally, you've been 'S.O.S.'ing' the inner for the past twenty-four hours in your deep anxiety. Let's have a seat in the West for a minute or two and you can tell me the entire story."

Geoff looked into the kindly, grandfatherly face, let out a prolonged sigh and nodded once. He started at the best place to begin a story – the beginning - and then poured the whole thing, leaving nothing out all the way to the end. The old initiate nodded his understanding and encouraging the younger to unburden himself and to get all the anxiety out, to sort of put it on the table where they could look at it.

When Geoff had finished his narrative, the old man looked thoughtfully at him.

"Frater, I'm going to use my dispensatory authority and tell you a little bit about the ritual you hold in you hands. Even though it is above your grade, I feel I can trust your discrimination in this matter." He shifted his weight as he crossed one leg over the other.

"What you could not know is that many of the Greater Mystery rituals are designed to be enacted on the highly symbolic environment of the Inner Planes of Consciousness rather than in a physical temple like the ones you have encountered thus far in you career. The Ritual of the Three Ways is just such a document. It is so far beyond the experience of your would-be adversary who is used to playing at the magic of the Goetia that he has no concept of what he is dealing with.

"The 'Three Ways' is designed to awaken the subtler senses of a initiate to the inner levels of reality. In other words, it is used to develop clairvoyance or the 'Second Sight'. It is based upon a formula that was used in ancient Greece during the Eleusinian Mysteries.

During that initiation into the Greater Mysteries, the Candidate was sent out of his body onto the Astral Plane. The scenes encountered were symbolically represented in the after-death myths of the popular religion. What those outside the gates of the temple never realize is that the myths conceal initiatory formula. This is also true, by the way, of what is represented in both the Egyptian Book of the Dead (whose proper title is "The Book of the Coming Forth by Day) and the Tibetan Book of the 'Bardo Thodol'. The world of the afterlife is the Astral Plane and death is a symbol for initiation because we die to our old selves and are reborn into the higher awareness." He chuckled and went on, "I wonder what many of our more orthodox friends would do if they realized where their term 'born again' came from?

In those ancient mysteries of Greece the soul of the departed, that is the Candidate would approach the banks of the river Styx, which represented the lower astral and the dividing boundary between life and death. After paying the Ferryman to row him across the waters he would come to a crossroads and thus be presented with three choices, hence the title 'Three Ways'. Crossroads have always been considered very powerful places for this reason.

"The way to the left was the way to Tartarus, the place

of punishment. This is the place called Purgatory by the Roman Church, and is, in reality a state of consciousness where, after review of our incarnation, we burn away and adjust the balance of our Karma.

"The way to the right was the way to the Elysian Fields, and was the place of reward for the righteous. This is a state of consciousness where souls after balancing their karmic debt, would rest and prepare for the next incarnation."

"And what is the way straight ahead, the Middle-way, asked Geoff?

"The way of the initiate, which is the way of service. It is by this path that we learn how to become co-creators of our destiny.

"But Oscar, doesn't know about these choices does he, the old man continued. "I wonder which way he'll choose?"

What do you mean? You're going to let me give him the ritual?"

"He has reached a point in his path where he has asked for the opportunity to experience the crossroads. We don't think he is ready, but we are fallible, he might be. His higher self will judge his soul's mettle not us. He has declined, by his actions and attitude to be placed under our guidance. We will soon see what he is made of. And he will see that also," he added cryptically.

Remember what our Frater Francis Bacon wrote under the name of Shakespeare, "This above all: To Thy own self be true, and it must follow, as the night the day, Thou canst not be false to any man…"

* * * * *

Oscar was delighted when Geoff placed the manuscript in his hands. He then arrogantly showed his dark temple to his boyhood friend. All the while Oscar examined the instructions of performing the ceremony and trance work.

"This is surprisingly simple," Oscar said. "I don't see any reason to not try it out immediately."

"Don't underestimate its power or danger," Geoff warned his boyhood companion. "And don't over estimate your abilities"

Oscar sneered at him and simply said, "Get Out!"

Geoff walked out and to his car, which was parked in front of the house. Before he even left, Oscar had been arranging a couch in the temple for the trance. Geoff sat in his car, shaking his head, marveling at how the world had revealed the unsuspected flaws in his former friend's character. This had been so easy for him. I wonder which piece of knowledge he'll want me to steal from the archives next?

Just as he said this, he was paralyzed by an unholy shriek that came from the house in front he was parked. It was the sound that some have witnessed when they deal with a soldier who was suffering from posttraumatic shock begin reliving the horrors of the battle. It came from the very depths of hell, from seeing or experiencing something so horrible that the fragile house of personality was never, should never be expected to withstand it. Thus, it was the sound of the crumbling of the island of sanity that this house represented, crumbling into the darkness of chaos.

The door of the house was flung open to bang upon its hinges as Oscar, tearing at his hair, spittle dripping from the corner of his mouth, eyes wide in fear of a vision only he could see ran to the sidewalk. Geoff expected his friend to run to him, but it was if Oscar couldn't see him. He paused irresolutely on the sidewalk, screamed that horrible shriek again and then began running down the middle of the street, toward the center of lights that was Hollywood Boulevard.

Funny, reflected Geoff, the people he passed only gave him a moment's notice, as if this was a common occurrence in this neighborhood. Perhaps it was.

Geoff reentered the house and walked into the temple. He retrieved the book as he looked around in wonder. All of the furniture was smashed and overturned. The couch had been shredded. Strangest of all was there were clearly prints of a very large dog everywhere, especially upon the altar, which looked like it had been torn apart by savage teeth. Geoff looked up at a picture of the Egyptian God Annubis on the wall. A jackal?

Geoff elected to simply retrieve the Ritual and leave with out touching any thing else. He still had visions of Oscar's terror filled face as he madly rushed down into the very material lights of the boulevard below. He made his way back to the mansion with the book firmly tucked underneath his arm.

As he entered the library he was not surprised to find a reception committee awaiting him. Dr. Alexander, Rabbi Bergman and Frater Jacob all looked up sternly but not angrily as he entered and placed the document upon the table.

"Well Little Brother," said the Rabbi, " you have returned the ritual. That is good. But, don't you feel you owe us an explanation?"

For the second time in twenty-four hours, Geoff told his story, leaving nothing out. The assembled men listened with close attention and nodded encouragement. When he finished, he turned to Arthur and asked:

"Most Greatly Honored Frater, the look on Oscar's face was one of a man being haunted and hunted over the brink of madness. Did the ritual do that?"

"What your mysterious Frater in the Temple of

Initiation did not tell you is one of the first effects of opening your astral vision, especially with this ritual," he answered, pointing to the book on the table "is that you must meet the 'Guardian of the Ways'. Did it not occur to you odd that the path to inner awakening was completely unguarded? We meet our shadow at those crossroads, a vision of our naked soul. This is a stressful experience for the prepared consciousness of one of our initiates and constitutes a severe test. But for one like Oscar, who was both unprepared and tainted with the drives of greed, cruelty and power it would have been devastating. His shadow would have been terrifying indeed to behold. And once that door is opened, it cannot be forever fully closed again. Oscar will be haunted not only by the vision of that terrible wraith but will know on an intuitive level that, unless he completely transforms his character that shadow will be awaiting to greet him when he makes his transition at the end of this incarnation. In short, Oscar has now met the Dweller on the Threshold and that experience will walk with him, every moment for the rest of his life."

"But why didn't the older Frater tell me about the guardian?"

"Because it was not your test but Oscar's. He requested and was allowed to face the challenge. He'll not bother you anymore for this incarnation.

"Tell me more about the man in the white robe. You say he wore a Pentagram Lamen? What color?" "It was golden. Why?"

"The Golden Pentagram is the special symbol of the Steward or visible head of The Fraternity. There is only one Steward, Geoffrey," said Jacob. "And that person is Dr. Alexander who is old in comparison to you, but not the ancient you described."

"Wait a moment," said Arthur. "Geoff, my brothers, come with me for a moment."

The group, led by Alexander took the route to the Temple of the Lesser Mysteries, the same path that Geoff had made his escape on earlier that evening. But instead of entering the lodge room as Geoff and the others had expected, Arthur paused in the antechamber and pointed to the wall of photos.

Geoff stared at the aged photographs peering down at him. He pointed to one of them that showed a white haired and bearded man with twinkling eyes and said: "That's the old man. He was the one I talked to in the temple."

Arthur turned with a smile to his brethren. "It seems, my Fraters, that Geoff has made the acquaintance of our Most Greatly Honored Frater Josiah Albert Case. He served as Steward of all the temples of the Fraternity and Servant of the Light from 1878 to 1881. He died or made his transition in 1885.

OPEN THE GATES OF CHAOS

"I hate to cast a shadow on such a happy gathering, but I need to share something with you." The speaker was the Reverend Robert Evans, a bishop in the 'Old Catholic Rite,' and a member of the Fraternity. "I hope it may be due to the fact that we have just come through the choppy waters leading up to the Vernal Equinox, but perhaps it is more."

The happy occasion that the bishop referred to concerned me directly. It was a small dinner party held to celebrate my initiation earlier that evening into the mysterious organization so often referred to in these chronicles. Visions of the past few hours had presented themselves again and again to my mind, as if I were developing snap-shots in a darkroom. The images sprang to life with the vividness that recalled the original sensory intensity. The mechanics of ceremonial initiation have been distorted by hundreds of writers of occult thrillers who missed the mark, either because they were ignorant of the true nature of the principles of ceremonial and initiatory rituals, or because they simply wanted to increase the spectacular in their stories. The inner reality was more than impressive.

To put it simply, I was cast in the role of the protagonist in a drama portraying the soul's journey toward its awakening to its true potential and destiny. Sensory images of great power were planted into my garden of consciousness. Memories of being plunged into a path of unimaginable darkness and in the midst of this darkness of being challenged as to my preparedness and motives were still fresh. Still echoing in my memory was the thundering of a voice that forbade me to enter this inner life until I could offer myself in dedication to the unfoldment and manifestation of the Light through steadfast, unselfish service. Only then was I allowed to enter the Halls of Wisdom. Then came the experience of the near blinding light as I was brought forth from darkness to face clearly the symbolic representation of my higher self.

I knew that these symbolic seeds had been planted deep into my subconscious, their flowers to bloom forth, gloriously, at a later time, a time decreed by the Spirit residing in my heart. These images spun in my head as I shared a toast with Rabbi Bergman and Arthur. We placed the glasses upon the table as the good bishop approached us. Robert sat down in the chair proffered him by Arthur. I knew from previous conversations how much Arthur valued and respected his grace's psychic and intuitive capabilities. Thus it was not surprising that everyone's attention at the table became open and expectant.

"This morning," Robert continued, "as I was blessing the hosts and wine during the mass, I opened my attention to the inner, as I usually do, and I perceived something wrong – seriously wrong."

"Describe your perceptions carefully," Arthur requested.

"I felt strongly that there was a flaw in the weave of the astral substance," Robert said with a shrug of his shoulders.

Sean O'Leary, a friend of ours and a fellow traveler who also happened to be a detective with one of the local police forces, joined us just in time to hear the last of that comment. "I know what you mean, Bob," he commented. "The Telesmatic images weren't holding as well as normal last week when I was doing some personal work. I just put it down to it being the tail end of the dark cycle. Something is afoot, that's for sure."

"Not changing the subject," Bergman inserted, but have any of you ever heard the name Dr. Jeffrey Jenkins

"I have," I responded. "He's a professor of Near Eastern Archeology at a major university back east somewhere – or was until just recently. Some sort of minor scandal caused him to leave his post. Is that correct?"

"That's the man," answered Bergman with a nod and a pointed finger. "The rumors from good sources in the Brooklyn Chassidic community are that the good professor found something extremely rare, extremely valuable, and extremely interesting while researching the Vatican Catacombs last year.

"It seems our friend was doing some research that required the assistance of the Vatican Librarian. He had received permission to examine certain manuscripts stored in the chambers and caves that make up the Catacombs. As you all know, much of the collection still hasn't been cataloged. There is much undiscovered territory there. It is said that he was restricted to a certain area in the library, but by accident (at least, that was his claim), he got disoriented and ended up in another more restricted section. Here he found copies of many manuscripts that have been thought lost since the burning of the Library of Alexandria.

"He smuggled one of these out in the false bottom of his attaché case."

He smuggled it out under the noses of Vatican security?" asked Sean incredulously, his eyebrows rising. "What was it that he found?"

"An ancient book or scroll, I'm not sure exactly which. It deals with cosmology and magic. According to rumor, Jenkins made off with nothing less than the legendary Book of Gates." Bergman looked at Arthur knowingly. Arthur's eyes stared back, cold and unflinching, but he said nothing.

Robert let out a low whistle and said, "Ancient, indeed! Tradition says the Archangel Auriel, the angel who stands before the Gate of Darkness, gave that book to the human race in the most ancient of times. I always supposed that it was simply a legend, an invention, you know, like Lovecraft's Necronomicon."

"No," answered Arthur, "it's an actual and extremely

216

dangerous work that was thought to have been destroyed centuries ago. During one of my trips to Europe, when I was visiting our Lodge at Copenhagen, I was spending an afternoon with the archivist when I came across a bound manuscript purported to be a copy, a translation in English, of The Book of Gates. It was in vellum, bound in leather, about 36 by 26 inches, and about three inches thick. This copy was written by hand by no less a person than Dr. John Dee. I have a photocopy in my library at home that I copied from the one at the Copenhagen Lodge. Broadly, it postulates the existence of an incredibly vast but finite Universe – at least, this space/time continuum. That's incredible when you consider that this document is supposed to date from ancient times. Additionally, some of it seems to mirror theoretical concepts as modern as Hawkins, Talbot and Einstein."

"Einstein postulated that all space was curvilinear, I believe?" I asked.

"Well, the ancient Hindus certainly did. They called space 'Akasha,' and symbolized it by an indigo egg. Symbolically, the Universe is conceived as an egg-shaped island existing in a vast ocean of chaos, maintained by the mind of Deity. Perhaps there exists many, many more similar islands, each independent, each with their unique set of laws. At the four quarters of our universe, at its outer boundaries, the book in question describers four great watchtowers, placed there by God to guard this space-time continuum from invasion by the forces of chaos that dwell without. It further states that these watchtowers are guarded by vast archangelic consciousnesses who maintain vigil so that the chaotic entities inimical to our universe are locked without."

"It does sound a bit like Lovecraft's and Derleth's fantasy fiction, doesn't it?" commented Sean.

"Yes, there have been some who have suggested that Lovecraft may have tapped into the Akashic Records when he wrote his stories," commented Bergman.

"But I still don't see why you describe this book, or scroll, as dangerous work, Arthur," I questioned.

"Its danger proceeds from the fact that it contains certain ritualistic techniques for establishing a rapport with certain conscious inner world entities. These entities are properly of the nature of the realm of dwellers in chaos. As such, they are antagonistic to all who dwell in the Cosmos. Furthermore, the book outlines procedures for opening a channel of manifestation whereby these entities supposedly could exert a direct influence on this plane."

"This influence, Bergman continued, 'would be of an extremely malevolent nature, coming as close to hellish as any of the fundamentalists' descriptions."

"But why would anyone wish to assist these maniacs?" I asked.

"Usually these are the people that espouse the 'me first and the hell with everyone else' philosophy," Arthur grimaced. "They feel that these entities will bestow upon them special favors of power and wealth in gratitude for providing a channel of manifestation. In some cases, they believe they can control and direct the powers of these beings who dwell outside the Gates of Chaos."

"Robert, if someone has been experimenting with the Book of Gates, and has been thus tampering with the fabric of the Cosmos, the description of what you perceived as a flaw in the astral substance could just be the beginning symptom of something that could have disastrous repercussions."

Robert looked up at Arthur, "I wonder what the Invisibles would advise?"

"We need to consult with them, certainly," answered Arthur, nodding. "Gentlemen, could you please join me at my house a week from tonight, say about 7:30 p.m.?" All nodded their acceptance, and Arthur continued, "I'll contact our sorors Miriam and Selena to joint us then, if possible. They will be able to balance the overly male polarity of this group around the table and additionally, as Second Order members, they can act as seers, if necessary."

The seven of us gathered at Arthur's home the following week. As we all donned our robes, I reflected, looking at the surroundings, that unless one were to look closely at the books in Arthur's library, it would be hard to detect his interest (and knowledge) on esoteric things. I realized with a start, as we moved toward a door concealed behind some curtains on the far wall of his study, that I had never been through that door. In fact, I had never even noticed that it existed. My surprise must have been noticed, for Miriam turned to me and said with a smile, "Life sometimes appears different after initiation, Michael?"

Robert added, "Arthur has placed a glamour, a spell if you wish, upon that door. It's not that it becomes invisible; it's just that people don't notice that it's there. That is, those people who are not members of his spiritual family."

We passed, one by one, through the door. I found I was in a hallway perhaps twenty feet long, almost completely dark, save for two small alcoves on either side. A pedestal holding an egg and, on the other side, a human skull were spotlighted within these small alcoves - the symbols of life and death. As we proceeded through this corridor, I could just make out the glimmer of a flickering light in the room beyond. I emerged into this room, actually a chapel with a high ceiling, by passing through another doorway, over which was the symbol of a circled cross. On a low platform on three sides of the chapel were pews with high backs. In the middle of each of these was a small table, upon which was burning a votive candle in its appropriate elemental color. Beside each candle was one of the 'weapons' of the Tarot. On the eastern side of the chapel was a dais of three steps. Beyond its small elemental pedestal, there was an altar like one would find in a church. As Arthur raised the level of the lighting, I could better see the large wooden cross upon the wall above the altar, and observed that a large rose was crucified upon it. In the center of the temple was a double-cubical altar with four large throne-like chairs facing in toward it.

I immediately sensed a change in the atmosphere of this room. It was similar to what I had experienced in Chartres Cathedral and the King's Chamber of the Great Pyramid. I had been in each of them late at night, one of the benefits of having friends in the right places. When the chatter of the tourists died away, I became aware of a profound peace and sense of balance, and also an almost indefinable hum of great power. The sound seemed to come from everywhere at once. It was then that I realized that the source of this power was inside of me! This was exactly the sense I got as I entered Arthur's chapel and stood with my robed Fraters and Sorors in the dimly lit atmosphere, with the candles flickering and the smell of incense in the air.

Robert, Selena and Miriam had been selected to accompany Arthur on the Inner Planes to visit with the Inner Chiefs. These four moved forward and sat in the chairs; Arthur in the East, Robert in the South, Selena in the North, and Miriam in the West. The remaining three of us paced the circle; reinforcing the formidable seals and warding that were already in place in this sanctum. As I watched, Arthur and the other three flying souls assumed the god-form posture and proceeded to withdraw their focus of attention, stage-by-stage, to the inner. From each one in turn, I heard a sibilant hiss of air come from between their lips, and by this outward sign; I knew they now walked upon the inner, through the Court of the Seekers.

Those of us who remained maintained a vigilant watch. It promised to be a long wait, so we took turns at guard duty. One of us would nap while the other two stood sentry. Early the next morning, the sunrise found us all sitting around Arthur's swimming pool, enjoying a hearty breakfast of Belgian waffles, sausages, eggs, and strawberries.

 We had stood watch through the night. About two hours earlier, Arthur and his fellow travelers returned to their bodies. As the four gathered together to write their records and compare notes, the remaining three of us closed down the temple, releasing the seals and warding we had set the evening before. The four retired to various couches and bedrooms to get some well-deserved though brief rest, while Sean and I invaded Arthur's kitchen to create the hearty cholesterol-laden feast we were all now enjoying.

Arthur sat quietly comparing the four write-ups of the inner planes conference, looking for any inconsistencies, enhancing and clarifying various points. He put down his pen and sat back with a heavy sigh:

"There is trouble in river City, my friends."

Arthur outlined the counsel they had received from the Third Order. Jenkins had indeed acquired a copy of the infamous Book of Gates. His purpose from the beginning of his well-thought-out plan, covering a period of over ten years, was to open one of the Gates in order to make a pact with an entity from without. He felt this pact would provide him with unlimited power, in exchange for which he would provide this being with an avenue of expression into the Cosmos. He felt that he would be able to control this creature of chaos by using a magical weapon, the legendary blasting rod of Hermes Trismegistus. The last time this mysterious object had been seen was in the possession of the famous Rosicrucian Chief, P.B. Randolph, shortly after the Civil War. Frater Randolph's tomb was in New Orleans, and three of us were to be chosen by Tarot divination to journey there.

The cards were cut. The first was Key 5 of the Trumps, The Hierophant. Robert looked up and nodded his acceptance. The second card cut was the Hermit, the 9th Key, and the Adept. It was no surprise that all knew that this referred to Arthur. The third Key cut was the Knight of Cups, the young Quester. As this was unclear, Bergman cut a fourth card – The Fool!

"The Neophyte," Bergman grunted. "Evidently the powers that be have selected you, Michael, our newest traveler, to go on this quest."

*   *   *   *   *

When we arrived in the romantic city at the mouth of the great river we agreed that we would visit nearby Tulane University the next morning. There we consulted with the Assistant Chairperson of the History Department, Dr. Winter Brown, about the local legends connected with P.B. Randolph and the legendary rod.

Dr. Brown was a strikingly attractive woman in her mid-forties. Her long auburn hair, drawn close at the nape of her neck, as beautiful as it was, still came in second place to her startling green eyes that would gaze steadily back at you with the force of consciousness that seemed to say, "here is a person not to be underestimated."

"P.B. Randolph was an amazing man," she answered with a dazzling smile. "He was a personal friend of President Lincoln, and spent many nights at the White House. At the same time, he was a close acquaintance of the Confederate General Albert Pike of Masonic fame. There is even a story that names these three individuals as the ruling triad in America of that ever-elusive Rosicrucian organization. Randolph and Pike were known to be good friends with the French Adept and writer on occult subjects, Alphonse Constant."

"Alphonse Constant," I mused. "Why isn't that name familiar to me?"

"Probably because he is almost always referred to by his pen name, Eliphas Levi," answered Arthur.

"Eliphas Levi!" I exclaimed. "The author of Transcendental Magic. That's where I remember reading about the blasting rod."

"Yes," Dr. Brown said, nodding. "Levi evidently knew about the rod of power, for he describes it in detail in his book on magic."

"But as is characteristic of Levi," interrupted Arthur, "he left out important details and inserted blinds. He also gives the impression in the book that the rod was an implement that anyone could manufacture, which is certainly not the case. This rod, or wand, comes down from very ancient times. Legend, as narrated in the secret archives of certain esoteric orders, states that it was this instrument of incredible power that the Manu of the Atlantian Age, Narada, used to open the Elemental Gates, bringing about the final cataclysm that drowned that continent when they had descended too far into the evil of the left-hand path.

"What happened to it after the fall of Atlantis, Dr. Alexander?" asked Dr. Brown with obvious interest.

"The same legends say that Narada entrusted the weapon to the young priest, Helios, who in turn conveyed it to Narada's successor, Melchizedek, who carried it with the Seed bearers to the Nile Delta and the plains of Giza. It was said to have been placed in the tomb of Melchizedek or Hermes, as he had come to be known. It remained there for millennia, until the young

Macedonian conqueror, Alexander, entered the Tomb in search of it.

"The story goes that when Alexander broke the seal and entered the antechamber, he was confronted by an amazing sight. Mysterious glowing lamps, lamps that must have been burning for thousands of years, illuminated the chambers. Across the chamber, flanking a small alcove, were the statues of two winged sphinxes, approximately the size of a man. The eyes of these statues were of some strange gems, and they stared at each other – or, actually, at a point halfway between them. Suspended at this point in empty space was the blasting rod! It is said that Alexander inched slowly forward in almost hypnotic fascination. As he moved to observe how the rod was able to float with no visible support, he inadvertently moved between one of the statues and the rod, evidently breaking some energy beam. The rod immediately fell to the sandy floor of the chamber. Simultaneously, the glowing lamps extinguished, leaving him in the flickering darkness of the torch with which he had entered."

"Alexander reached cautiously forward and picked up the rod, perhaps expecting that it might bite! As he drew the weapon to him in wonderment, he became aware of glowing figure of a man dressed in the robes of the high priest of Thoth standing before him. Alexander was sure he was seeing a ghost, but in tribute to his legendary courage (or arrogance, depending on your view of him), he stood and saluted the apparition, using the sign of an initiate that had been taught to him by his teacher,

Aristotle. To his amazement, the figure returned the salute and spoke to him by name.

"Hail to thee, Alexander, son of Phillip of Macedonia, mind son of Aristotle, spiritual son of Apollo. Welcome to the land of Khem. I am called Thoth Hermes. You hold now in your hand great power. I ask you to take this statement of wisdom to guide your use of it."

"With these words, Hermes vanished; but in the place where he had appeared was a stele or stone table of shiny, bright green color. The young conqueror picked up the tablet and read the following:

Truth, without falsehood, certain and most true, that which is above is as that which is below, and that which is below is as that which is above, for to perform the miracles of the One Thing. From One do all things originate. By One are all mediated. All things have their birth from this One Thing by adaptation. Its Father is the Sun. Its Mother is the Moon. The Wind carries it in its belly. The Earth is its nurse. This is the father of all perfection, or consummation of the whole world. It is integrating if it is turned into earth.

Separate the earth from the fire, the subtle from the gross, suavely, and with great ingenuity. It ascends from earth to heaven and descends again to earth. Hence it gains or receives the powers of the greater and lesser. So thou has the glory of the whole world; therefore let all obscurity vanish before thee. This is the strong force of all forces, overcoming every subtle and penetrating every solid thing. Thus were the worlds created. Thus were all wonderful adaptations after this manner. Therefore I am called Thrice Greatest Hermes, and have the three components of the total philosophy of the world. I have completed what I have to tell concerning the Operation of the Sun."

"After the death of Alexander several years later, the rod and tablet were carried to Alexandria with the body of the young Macedonian. The tablet was placed in the Library. It was believed that the Rod of Hermes was buried with Alexander. It surfaced briefly during the late fifteenth century in Toledo, Spain, only to disappear once again. Rumor has it that it migrated to Florence with the expulsion of the Qabalists in 1492. It was among the many items that were brought back to Paris during the sack of Florence by the Grand Army of Napoleon. There is remained until the mid 1800's, when Eliphas Levi came into its possession."

"That's a fascinating story, Doctor," smiled Analia, "and you told it in such intimate detail."

"Well," Arthur responded, "Alexander holds a special interest for me. This history is based mostly upon legend, yet I have found that these old traditions usually have a basis in fact. Haven't you had that experience, Doctor?"

"Indeed, I have," answered Dr. Brown. " You don't

mind if I borrow liberally from your narrative when I lecture on Alexander the Great next time?" They both chuckled.

"As for the question of whether the rod was actually buried with Mr. Randolph," continued Dr. Brown, "I think we will have to leave that to conjecture. You see, here in New Orleans, all burials are above ground in vaults. This is necessary because the water table is so near the surface. Mr. Randolph's final resting place was moved about forty years ago, just a few feet, actually, because of erosion. During the short period of time while the casket was disinterred and was kept in the mortuary, there was an incident of vandalism. The vandals were caught in the act of opening the coffin. When questioned, they admitted to seeking to steal 'magical' artifacts. They failed to find anything unusual. In point of fact, if there ever was a blasting rod, it apparently was not buried with our famous friend."

After we left Dr. Brown and were walking across Tulane and Loyola's bordering campuses, I admitted to the others that I was somewhat baffled:

"If the Third Order knew that the rod wasn't here, why didn't they tell us?"

"While the Third Order knows much more than we do," answered Robert, "they are far from being omniscient."

"Besides," commented Arthur, "when one door closes, another invariably opens. They'll assist us. All we have to do is remain receptive and patient."

We boarded the streetcar and returned to the French Quarter, where our hotel was located. The trolley was passing Lee's Circle when Robert spoke up. "If it's all right with both of you, I'd like to visit St. Louis's Cathedral this afternoon."

We agreed, and when the streetcar reached Canal Street, we disembarked and crossed it, heading down Royale in the direction of the French Market and Jackson Square. I'd always loved New Orleans and in particular the French Quarter with its wrought iron railings, narrow cobblestone streets, and abundance of interesting establishments. As we threaded our way through the crowds, past Pat O'Brien's and Pete Fountain's, I reflected upon the serious nature of our quest and the contrast of the happy, light-hearted expressions upon the tourists' faces around us. Finally we reached Jackson's square, with its statue of Andrew Jackson and sidewalk artists. Bordering it stood the old Cathedral, next door to the Civil War Museum.

As we entered the big doors of the Cathedral, we could hear a hymn being sung. It was the old standard, "A Mighty Fortress is Our God." When they came to the line, "This body they may kill, God's truth abideth still, His Kingdom is forever…" I turned and saw a most peculiar look on Arthur's face. I asked him if everything was okay? He looked like he had seen a ghost. He replied that he had had a premonition, but declined to talk about it further.

As we stood in the small group at the rear of the worshippers listening to the choir, a small Black woman slipped beside Arthur and said to him in a thick Cajun accent:

"Please, he said he'd like for you to come to him soon." She pressed a book into his hand and, before any of us could question her further, she turned and disappeared through the door.

Arthur, Robert and I looked in vain across the milling crowd that had filled the square.

"What do you make of that?" the bishop asked.

"Maybe the clue rests here," Arthur answered, holding up the book. It was an inch-thick paperback, Voodoo in New Orleans, by Richard Tallant. A silk ribbon marked a page in the introduction where several paragraphs had been underlined. Arthur read them without comment, and then passed the book to us.

The underlined text narrated a story about how the author had encountered a young Voodoo priest in an occult supply shop on Rampart Street. It told of the incredible magnetic power possessed by the young man's presence and which especially seemed to radiate from his eyes.

"Well, what do you think?" I asked.

"The young man in the story would have white hair now. That encounter took place at least thirty years ago," answered Robert.

Arthur, who had been standing quiet still, gazing up at the rose window of the church, suddenly spoke:

"We need to go to the shop on Rampart. It is the next step upon our quest." With this surprising statement, he set forth with a long stride across the quarter, leaving both Robert and I struggling to keep up.

Arthur would periodically stop and ask for directions, referencing the book in his hand. To our surprise and irritation, we found ourselves being directed away from the area where we knew the shop must be located.

After a few of these misleads, we stopped in front of Preservation Hall, the old concert hall where old men assemble every evening bearing instrument cases of assorted types and shapes. They pull their trumpets, clarinets, and other instruments out and proceed to play the best Dixieland in the world. These halls had heard the immortal music of some of the greatest talents in the genre, including 'Gabriel' himself, Louis Armstrong. As the sounds of this unique music wafted our way, Arthur spoke to us:

"It seems, my friends, that this man's reputation is widespread here in the Quarter. Also, there is a conspiracy, not an organized conspiracy, but a conspiracy nevertheless, to misdirect our quest for him.

We know that his place is on Rampart Street; therefore, I suggest that we move in that direction.

When we finally reached Rampart Street, Arthur questioned someone who had the look of a resident or one who worked in the neighborhood. The person pointed to the right and, to everyone's astonishment (especially the old man he had asked), we turned to the left. Twice more Arthur stopped someone and inquired about directions. Invariably the person would point back the way we had come. Common sense would tell us that we should go that way, but Arthur would resolutely press on in the opposite direction. With the third "guide," we knew Arthur had been correct in his assumption of misdirection by the local inhabitants. He approached a woman who could only be described as a bag lady, produced the book and asked for directions. The woman's eyes got large as she retreated back a step. She began giving Arthur detailed instructions, ending up by telling us that it was close to the Cathedral! As she left, Robert pointed excitedly across the street. There stood the shop, advertising "voodoo, curios, charms."

We all laughed, and shaking our heads, crossed over and entered the store. A small bell announced our arrival as we opened the door. The smell of incense hung in the air, and a small stuffed alligator hung from the ceiling. There were cases filled with talismans, coins, and charms of every type, and book cases lined the walls, featuring old paperback standards like The Sixth and Seventh Books of Moses," "Pow-Wows,"

"Albertus Magnus' Egyptian Secrets," "Lewis de Claremont's Incense, Herb and Oil Magic." We did not have long to look around before we all found our attention focused on the commanding presence of the old Black man who stepped through the curtained doorway that separated the store from the rooms in back.

"I see you penetrated the maze of superstition and found me," the old man stated matter-of-factly.

"You did send an invitation," responded Arthur, holding the book up by way of explanation.

"Yes, I knew," the man answered, a smile transforming his face, his eyes taking on a sparkle. "But if you had not been the right one – he who was chosen – you would have continued to go in circles ending at the Cathedral where you started. Such was the glamour I placed upon that book," he finished with a shrug of his stooped shoulders, displaying the palms of both hands as if to say, 'what else could I have done?'

"But that is now unimportant. My name is John. I can see you are the ones the Loas spoke to me about in my dreams."

After Arthur made our introductions, I asked John about the Loas.

"The Loas are the great inhabitants of the spirit world. They guide and watch over our affairs. They are the great forces of existence! They told me in my dreams that I should talk to one who comes seeking the flaming rod. I was confused at first, when the other man came to me asking about the rod.”

“You know where the blasting rod is?” asked Arthur.

“Indeed! We have been the guardians of the Wand of Hermes since the Adept Randolph entrusted it to my grandmother many years back.”

“You said another has come seeking it,” Robert interrupted?

“Yes, but he was not the right man,” answered our host.

“How did you know that?” I inquired.

“His aura did not bear the sign of initiation,” John said, suddenly very solemn. “The same sign my grandmother told me shone in the radiance of Randolph. The same sign that is in each of your auras!”

That this individual could discern a symbol in each of our auras did not surprise me. I had been told that one had, indeed, been placed there at my initiation, and the power radiating from John convinced me of his occult powers.

When we inquired more closely as to the appearance of the other man, John’s description convinced us that it must indeed have been Dr. Jenkins who had preceded us.

"What did you tell him concerning the blasting rod, John," Arthur asked?

"I claimed ignorance, and then tried to sell the gentleman some love incense or a small good luck charm. He became quite upset and stormed from my shop."

John motioned for us to come through the curtain to his quarters in the store. It was much like any small apartment: a bath, kitchenette, and combination living and bedroom. Two tall bookcases stood nearby, crammed full of books. He motioned us to follow him across the room to an alcove that was curtained off. As he drew back the curtain, we could see the presence of an altar of the Voudoon Religion. He knelt in front of this altar and removed a couple of loose floorboards. In the recess below rested a black leather case bearing on its lid mystic symbols, some familiar, and some unknown to me. Among the familiar was a gold cross bearing a five petaled Tudor rose.

John took this case and placed it upon his bed. Then he beckoned to Arthur. "Please, open it. Take the weapon," he instructed. "You will need it in your quest."

Arthur opened the case and gazed within, and immediately looked up at John with a questioning expression upon his face. John in turn frowned with concern, and turned the case around. I crowded forward and looked within. We all could see the red satin liner and the impression where the rod once had rested, but the blasting rod of Hermes Trismegistus was gone.

"He must have come back while I was away for dinner," John said. " I grossly underestimated the avarice of this Dr. Jenkins. It appears you must pursue your opponent, Dr. Alexander."

"Yes, but where," I mused aloud?

"In that matter I can be of some assistance," John rejoined. "You see, he borrowed my phone while he was here. He must have been in a hurry, for he left his notes on my note pad. Evidently he called the airport. See? Here is the number of the international terminal. And this word, what does it mean to you?"

We all looked at the word written on the pad amidst the scribbles and doodles. The word was "Alexandria. 8:00 p.m."

A quick check of the airline schedules revealed that an international flight departed for Cairo via Miami at 8 p.m. every evening. It would be a short hop then to fly into Alexandria, Egypt. Our opponent had a 48-hour head start. He had the additional advantage of knowing his destination. We were indeed playing catch-up.

Arthur turned to the Bishop. "Robert, wire Daoud to meet us at the Cairo Airport. Fill him in on the details as we know them, and tell him that the one who dwells within the Mystic Mountain requests his assistance. Alexandria is the site of many ancient power sites. Jenkins must plan to open the Gate there. He actually intends to open the Gate of Chaos."

Twenty-four hours later the three of us were flying over the Atlantic Ocean on our way to the ancient city of the mysteries. Daoud, I learned, was one of the Chiefs of the Cairo Lodge. He had readily assented to the request. When we touched down at the city of the pyramids, he was there to both welcome us and to usher us all onto a waiting aircraft, which took off for Alexandria minutes later. He was a medium height black man, appearing to be in his mid-forties. He wore a tee shirt and fatigue pants with sandals on his feet and a fez upon his head. Strange as this wardrobe might seem, upon him it looked perfectly natural.

Daoud explained that the ancient quarter of the city was a tangled mass of narrow streets, alleys, and dead ends. The exact location of many of the oldest ruins was usually a case of conjecture, rather than certain knowledge; however, the most likely location where Jenkins would attempt to perform the operation, would be the site of the Temple of Hypatia. The Order archives revealed that it was located in a certain section of the city.

Like most ancient cities, Alexandria was layered. Present-day structures were not only built out of the stones of prior structures, but on top of the foundations of the past. Cemeteries would even be found on top of ancient tomb yards. Once again, we were at a disadvantage. Jenkins evidently already knew the location of Temple. Where or how could we hope to find that information?

We attempted a search during the few hours that remained to us before sundown. It was like threading our way through a maze. We soon decided that we would break off our search until the morning and retire to our hotel for a late dinner and a rest.

That night, I had the strangest dream. I walked the moonlit streets of Alexandria's old quarter, I was dressed in my robes of an initiate. The whole dreamscape seemed to glow in the moonlight. As I half floated, half walked down one of the twisted streets, I came to a courtyard with a small fountain. Across the courtyard, I saw what appeared to be a small church. In front of this church were two obelisks, each bearing Egyptian hieroglyphics. Instead of the conventional cross or crucifix, there was an ankh over the door. I had only a moment to observe this, for my attention was drawn to a woman robed and veiled in white, carrying a staff in the shape of the Caduceus of Hermes. She beckoned for me to follow, and disappeared within the church. I rushed to the door, afraid that I had lost her. As I entered the rear of the church, I could see that she had glided to the front of the sanctuary, where she stood beside the altar. An ankh was displayed on the front of the table.

I walked towards her as she pointed repeatedly to the

altar. "What are you trying to tell me?" I asked.

In answer, she once again pointed at the altar and shouted, "Hypatia."

I bolted awake with that word ringing in my ears. It took a moment before I realized that I had shouted the word. Robert, Daoud and Arthur were beside me in seconds with concern on their faces.

"Frater, are you alright," asked Robert? "You called out."

I recounted my dream to them.

"Perhaps we have had assistance from the Inner Planes," suggested Arthur. He paused and continued. "A woman dressed as you described would fit the description of a priestess of Alexandria. More exactly, the Caduceus of Hermes was only carried by the High Priestess of the Alexandrian Mysteries. Coupled together with the word, or rather, name upon your lips when you awakened, I would venture to guess that you had a vision of Hypatia, the last great hierophant and high priestess of the Mysteries of Alexandria."

"I know that church with the obelisks and ankhs that you have described," interjected Daoud.

"You mean there really is such a church," I asked in disbelief?

"Oh, yes, my brother. The ankh is also known as the

Coptic Cross. The place you described, complete with courtyard and fountain, and is one of the oldest Coptic Christian churches in all of Egypt."

The hour approaching midnight as we set forth once again, through the old quarter in the direction of the Coptic Church, in hopes that we would find a clue to the location of the Temple of Hypatia and the critical Gate to the Other World. As we drove closer and closer, I began to experience the feeling of déjà vu. I recognized this street. I had been this way. When we reached the courtyard of the small church it appeared different from my dream only because now the buildings were not glowing.

We hurried to the door, wondering how we would gain admission at this time of night. We needn't have been concerned, however, for the door was ajar. We approached the altar and stopped. It appeared to be a dead end.

Arthur spoke. "Many times these altars are built over older altars. Just where did Hypatia point on the altar in your dream, Michael?"

"Towards the back panel," I answered.

"Look," Daoud said. "Look at these marks on the floor." He pointed to scratches on the floor, just behind the rear of the altar.

"It looks as if something scraped across this part of the

floor," observed Robert. "It swings out in a half circle, like a door. Do you think that the altar can be moved?"

"I doubt it," Arthur answered. "It looks very substantial, but, perhaps…" he started feeling along the underside of the altar. We all leaned forward expectantly, but nothing happened.

Not to be discouraged, Arthur knelt down and peered at the surface of the altar. "Ah, just like in the old Sherlock Holmes' stories," he exclaimed as he reached forward and pushed the carving of the Ankh on the panel. With a loud metallic click, the rear panel popped open about an inch. Arthur pulled the panel the rest of the way out, revealing a stairway descending through a hole in the floor underneath the altar.

Before we could congratulate him on his discovery, we began to feel a strong wind howling up from the stairs, and with it came an eerie keening wail.

 "Oh God! What is that," I asked?

"The sounds of chaos, I hope we're not too late," Arthur replied.

We all scrambled down the long flight of stairs, and then down a long corridor. We emerged into another passageway that intersected at right angles to the first. As we passed into this second corridor, I stepped upon a carved ankh in the floor. At once the walls and floor started to tremble, and sound like distant rolling thunder rumbled all around us as a slab of solid sandstone slid into place, closing off our avenue of retreat. Robert, Arthur and I were on one side of this barrier with Daoud on the opposite side. He called, concern filling his voice, asking if we were okay. He then stated he would try to find some way to open this door. Arthur explained that it was imperative that we push on as quickly as possible, and for him to follow when he could.

The walls of the corridor had assumed a Greco-Egyptian aspect with paintings and lotus-crowned pillars on either side at measured intervals. The figures depicted on the walls jumped out at us when our flashlights illuminated them as we proceeded cautiously, wary of any other hidden triggers or traps. The keening wail, halfway between a siren and a cry of despair, was louder, and swept through us like the sound of a jet engine on a flight line. The wind blew at our hair, alternately blowing one way and then the other, like the snoring of a great giant.

Suddenly we emerged into a large room, flanked on either side by large lotus capital pillars. There we saw Dr. Jeffrey Jenkins, but we hardly recognized him. He was dressed in the robes of a high priest of the Mysteries of Thoth. The robes were flapping wildly in the wind. When he saw us, he laughed hysterically in a high pitch, spittle running down his chin.

"Behold! Our sacrifice has arrived!" he cried, pointing at us.

As I looked to see to whom he spoke, the pit of my stomach dropped away. What I can only describe as a hole in space whirled between two columns in the old temple. The wailing and wind issued from this source, as well as pool of undulating, glowing, noxious smelling green slime. What was even more horrifying was the certitude (don't ask me how we knew) that this slime possessed intelligence. But the intelligence was so totally alien and evil and purposefully malignant that even at our relatively distant proximity it jarred and battered our consciousness.

"Quick, everyone," shouted Arthur over the noise. "Use the Qabalistic Cross and seal your auric egg."

Only with forced concentration did we find will power enough to trace the cross upon ourselves, touching our brow and intoning the words "Ateh, Malkuth, Ve-Geburah..." As we intoned the final "Amen," I could feel that a barrier had been erected between that terrible essence of putrefying chaos and what I now remembered was the vehicle of my soul. I found myself repeating the words of the hymn that we had heard in New Orleans: "...A mighty fortress is our God..." But when I got to the part about "this body they may kill," I suddenly froze, considering our possible fate. To be seduced by that dweller of the gate would possibly preclude the gentle release of death! It would condemn one to be totally disintegrated, or else to dwell in non-time, non-Cosmos – forever.

Jenkins looked in our direction with a vacant stare. He

held a large, partially unrolled parchment scroll in one hand, and in the other, a wand. It had a clear crystal in one end, and a jet-black stone in the other. Suddenly his eyes snapped into focus.

"You fools!" he shouted. "I don't know who you are, but the fact that you are here is indication enough for me and my brother, here, that you are antagonistic to our plans – our vision. Do you think that you, with your puny knowledge, could thwart the day of return? My reign of triumph is almost here. He laughed again that high-pitched hysterical laugh, and this time, the keening wail laughed with him!

"Jenkins," Robert called, "for the love of God, don't you see what is awaiting at that infernal gate?"

"Your God? The God you believe in is invisible, intangible, imaginary. My God, your new god, is going to come through that portal, and there will be a real presence. Nothing remote about him! Look, he is coming even now. Closer and closer."

Sure enough, I could see an abomination starting to form. It was impossible to focus on it clearly, for it seemed to shift, flickering in and out of existence, changing second by second. From what I could see, I was glad that I could not see it clearly!

"Those idiots in Rome knew nothing of the power they possessed in this scroll. The Ancients knew! I know! And this knowledge is power indeed." Jenkins was screaming, spittle flying from his lips, the wailing and wind buffeting him.

Suddenly, a gust of the wind caught at the scroll. Jenkins reacted reflexively and somehow lost his grip upon the blasting rod. It rolled down his leg as he frantically tried to regain it. After striking his foot, it skidded away from him across the floor, spinning crazily all the way to the far side of the temple. Immediately the wailing ceased and, in its place, a sound halfway between a low growl and a gibbering chatter issued forth from the one forming there. The scroll Jenkins was clutching as he turned trembling towards the portal burst into flames. His eyes grew wide with terror as his mouth opened in a strangled scream, for there, coming through the Gate, was misty tentacle, like that of an enormous squid, except around each sucker were razor teeth that dripped a yellow steaming slime.

The tentacle worked its way towards Jenkins, who tried to escape. The snakelike appendage herded him into a space against a pillar, and wrapped itself about him. He screamed and fainted as the terror rapidly pulled him towards the opening.

Arthur leapt forward, brandishing his krill dagger that he had been carrying in a scabbard along his back. Another tentacle reached out for him, but as it sought to grasp his leg, he cut down with the wavy blade. This brought a howl from the creature as it knocked Arthur off the ground, sailing him across the hall to land at our feet. Jenkins had disappeared with an obscene sucking sound into the void. Now the tentacle sought its revenge against Arthur, who lay broken, bleeding and unconscious upon the floor.

As the dweller half emerge through the opening, two giant winged warriors, glowing with power, materialized and interposed between Arthur and the creature. They stood nine feet tall, one with flaming red hair and beard, dressed in crimson, the other with a dark beard and hair, dressed in dark scarlet.

"My God," I asked, "Who are they?"

Robert answered with awe in his voice, "Our God indeed has sent them. They are Archangels! The one with the red beard and flaming sword can only be the Great Michael."

"And the other?" I whispered?

"He can only be the Light-bearer – he who is called fallen – Lucifer!"

"Why is he here?" I gasped.

It was Michael who answered. "My brother and I serve the self-same God as you. The office of 'choice-giver' entrusted to him is as much a power of the Cosmos as is mine, or any of my brothers or sisters." A look of kinship passed between them as they turned and faced the now retreating abomination at the Gate. Lucifer and

Michael together pointed their swords at the vortex that whirled on the other side of the room, and both intoned a name of four syllables. Immediately, a flash of light went forth and closed the Gate and, I swear I saw a great finger, veiled in the blazing light, come from behind us and seal the portal with the symbol of an equal-armed, circled cross.

The two archangels turned, smiled, and nodded to us. Then they were gone.

At once we knelt at the side of Arthur. He was moaning softly, his body bruised, probably more than a few bones broken, and possibly suffering from a concussion. We had to get him to a doctor immediately, and our only way out was still blocked by a two-ton slab of sandstone. Just then a light came bobbing from across the temple, and Robert and I stiffened until we heard Daoud's voice.

As we quickly explained the situation, he looked at Arthur with concern. Indeed, all of us had tears in our eyes as we knelt by our friend. Daoud explained that he had been unable to open the door, and had doubled back to one of the intersecting tunnels and found another way into the temple. Evidently this was the way Jenkins had entered, for just a short distance away, he had found some tools, including two long poles. He hurriedly retrieved them and, taking our shirts off, we made an emergency stretcher and gently laid Arthur upon it.

Following Daoud's lead, we carried Arthur out the other

way. Sure enough, at the intersection of another tunnel we found Jenkins' tools. A lighted torch he had left there flickered in a breeze. Following this breeze, we emerged from an ancient mausoleum into the star strewn sky. Minutes later, after we had eased Arthur into the back of the van, Daoud drove us to a hospital.

After Arthur had been installed in his room with multiple contusions, a broken arm and leg, several broken ribs, and a mild concussion, I commented on how the premonition Arthur had experienced while listening to the hymn had almost come true. Robert stated that sometimes it did require a sacrifice of personal safety – someone who was willing to put their all on the line – before the higher powers could intervene.

"Did you notice," he continued, "how the Archangels were unable to take an active part until Arthur had directly confronted the dweller from without?"

"But he wasn't very effective, was he?" Daoud asked.

"I don't know about that," Robert countered. "Michael, did you see the finger that traced the circled-cross that sealed the hole in the chaos?"

Glad to have that vision confirmed, I admitted that I had.

"Did you hear the voice?"

"No," I answered frankly, "I did not. What did it say?"

Robert looked at the sleeping form of Arthur, then into the distance. Finally he looked again at Daoud and me. "It was a quote from the Bible," he explained again looking at Arthur, "It was directed at Arthur. I distinctly heard the voice whose finger healed the wound of the Cosmos tell Arthur, 'Thou hast done well, good and faithful servant.'"